___THE___
Lucky
Ones

THE
Lucky
Ones

Stephanie Greene

Greenwillow Books
An Imprint of HarperCollins*Publishers*

My heartfelt thanks to Jane Resh Thomas, Ron Koertge, Tim Wynne-Jones, and Rita Williams-Garcia for their generous support and encouragement in the writing of this book, and to my graduating class at Vermont College for their friendship.

The Lucky Ones

The text of this book is set in 12-point Venetian 301.
Book design by Paul Zakris.

Library of Congress Cataloging-in-Publication Data

Greene, Stephanie.
The lucky ones / by Stephanie Greene.
p. cm.
"Greenwillow Books."
Summary: During their annual summer vacation at her grandfather's home, Cecile hopes for their usual idyllic holiday, but with her sister growing up, her brother away at a summer job, and her parents fighting, nothing is as she envisions.
ISBN 978-0-06-156586-1 (trade bdg.) — ISBN 978-0-06-156587-8 (lib. bdg.)
[1. Family life—New York (State)—Fiction. 2. Brothers and sisters—Fiction. 3. Conduct of life—Fiction. 4. Friendship—Fiction. 5. New York (State)—Fiction.] I. Title.
PZ7.G8434Lu 2008   [Fic]—dc22   2007045085

First Edition 10 9 8 7 6 5 4 3 2 1

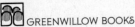 GREENWILLOW BOOKS

FOR R.W.C.

They were two little girls, six and eight. They were sisters.

"Not like that," said the older girl. She clutched her arm more tightly around her sister's neck to hold their two bodies close together. "I put my foot down first and say 'ooh!'" She stomped her bare foot on the gravel driveway for emphasis. "Then you put your foot down and say 'ah!'" She slapped her little sister's leg. "Go on, do it."

The younger girl stomped her bare foot on the gravel and said, "Ah!"

"Right," said the older girl. "Now wrap your arm around me the way I've got mine around you." The little girl did it. Their two heads pressed together, one blonde and straight, the other dark and curly.

"Okay," said the older girl. "First me, then you. Then me, then you, right?"

"Right."

"Ready?"

"Ready."

"One . . . two . . . three . . . go! Ooh!" said the older girl, taking a step.

"Ah!" said the younger obediently, stomping hard.

"Ooh!"

"Ah!"

"Ooh! Ah! Ooh, ah, ooh, ah, ooh, ah, ooh, ah!"

A seagull flying overhead, looking down, would have seen a strange two-headed, two-armed, four-legged creature hotfooting its way along the gravel driveway that led from the dock to the huge white house sitting under the elms. A giggling two-headed creature that staggered and stumbled from side to side until it reached the stone pillars at the head of the driveway, then suddenly broke apart as the two little girls collapsed on the lawn. They rolled onto their backs and planted the soles of their hot feet in the cool grass to soothe them, laughing up at the sky.

Later that night, when the clouds that had been banking on the horizon all afternoon delivered one of the rare storms the Island witnessed during July, Cecile, the younger sister, would scramble across the bedroom floor to her sister's bed at the first clap of thunder. Sleepily, Natalie would lift a corner of her blanket so Cecile could slip under, where she curled up against her sister's body and fell fast asleep. Happy as bear cubs in their cave, they were.

Chapter One

Things would be better when they got to Gull Island. Her parents couldn't possibly stay as icy to each other as they had been since their argument about Harry a few nights ago. And Natalie would stop sulking about the party she hadn't been allowed to go to once she claimed the canopy bed in the bedroom at the end of the upstairs hall at Granddad's. No, before that, even. When they got to the bridge.

No one was ever in a bad mood on Gull Island, Cecile told herself confidently, squashed in the middle of the back seat of the Thompson's pink station wagon as it sped along the flat highway toward the eastern end of Long Island. There was a harmony among them there that didn't exist in any other place. Let her mother and father do their end-less rounds of country-club dances and dinner par-ties and golf. The rules that governed the children's lives at home—from meals to washing to bedtime—would grow wonderfully lax. For one whole month, Cecile could go to the dock whenever she wanted, or lie on the beach, or go clamming or swimming—the whole island would be hers. She could smell the lavender soap in their bathroom in Granddad's house now, and the sheets on her bed that smelled like the fresh out-of-doors because Sheba hung them on the line in the drying yard all day.

Cecile could hardly wait to see Sheba. She wished they could eat in the kitchen with Sheba every night. Silly formal dining room with its silly rules. She'd help Sheba pick fresh flowers every day and make potpourri again from the petals of the roses in Granddad's garden. She wasn't going to worry about Harry, or her parents, or Natalie; she absolutely wasn't. Imagine a father being jealous of his own son, the way Natalie said their father was. Natalie seemed to hate everyone in their family these days. Cecile wasn't going to think about it.

If only the air in the car didn't feel so strained. She was going to explode into a million pieces if they didn't get there soon, and it would serve Natalie right. Horrible Natalie, who'd held herself pressed against the door for the entire ride so her skin wouldn't touch Cecile's, as if Cecile's skin was contaminated. Natalie didn't like it when anyone touched her, really, but Cecile knew she hated it most when it was her. The only times Natalie had looked at her for the entire ride was when their thighs had touched; then she shot Cecile a look of malice as she rubbed her perfect, tanned skin.

"Harry's not here, so I'm the oldest," Natalie had said, claiming a window the minute they got in the car. She'd refused to move, forcing Cecile to crawl over her without arguing. In the Thompson family pecking order, the oldest always got the window.

Jack got the other window even though he was the second youngest; he got carsick and needed air. A few years ago, when they'd been on their way home from church, Jack had announced he was going to be sick.

"You'll be fine as soon as we get home," their mother had said firmly, as if her voice could make even Jack's stomach behave. Jack promptly threw up. It splattered Natalie's dress and Cecile's shoes.

No one had disputed his right to a window seat ever since, which meant that for the past three hours, Cecile had been stuck in the middle with Lucy. As usual, she would have said, if anyone had been willing to listen. When the children abruptly rocked and swayed for about the hundredth time as Mr. Thompson swerved to pass the car ahead of theirs, Cecile longed to rest her head against the glass the way Natalie was doing.

Really, it wasn't fair. Ever since Natalie had turned fourteen, she'd been all pins and needles; Cecile was her favorite pincushion. It had hurt her feelings terribly at first. The day last winter when Natalie had stormed into Cecile's room without notice and knocked everything off her dresser with one sweep of a furious arm, Cecile had run in tears to her mother.

It wasn't because of her, Cecile's mother

explained, or even anything Cecile had done, really. It was because Cecile and Natalie were too close in age. "You're nipping at her heels" was how her mother put it, but, "She nips at mine, too," Cecile sniffed.

"It's not the same. You're not in as big a rush as Natalie."

"Where's she rushing to?" Cecile asked.

"That's exactly what I mean."

It added insult to injury, to have her mother sound so amused. It did nothing to soothe Cecile's hurt feelings, either, to be patted on the head as if she were a puppy and to have her mother put an end to the conversation by saying, "I count on you to be in a good mood."

Cecile had had to take what consolation she could from knowing her mother counted on her. But it was hard work being in a good mood all the time, especially when Natalie never even tried. The worse Natalie acted, the more she got away with. Maybe she wouldn't bother trying to be so good from now on, Cecile thought mutinously as she attempted to stretch her long legs in the limited space in front of her. It looked a lot easier to be bad.

When Mr. Thompson swerved right again, Natalie turned to her and said, "Your skin touched mine," and pulled her thigh away from Cecile's with both hands.

"I can't help it," Cecile said. "I don't have any room."

"You disgust me," said Natalie.

"You disgust me, too."

Quick and cool as a cat, Natalie reached out and scratched her. Cecile covered the two angry red lines that sprang up on her thigh and cried, "Mom! Natalie scratched me!"

"Knock it off," her father said testily, eyes straight ahead. She could have been bleeding to death, for all he cared.

"Girls?" Her mother reached back to cover Cecile's hands with one of her own and gave them a tiny shake of her head. Natalie sighed loudly and pressed her forehead against the window again. "When's the dance at the club this year?" Natalie asked sulkily, as if she might just allow the right answer to lure her out of her bad mood.

"I don't know. You'll have to ask Granddad." Mrs. Thompson patted Cecile's hand and smiled at her encouragingly. "Let Lucy rest her head on your shoulder, there's a good girl," she said before she turned back around. "And do something about your hair."

"Why? What's wrong with it?" Cecile asked as Lucy's sleepy head fell against her arm.

"It's a mess, as usual," Natalie muttered into the glass.

"It's not as if anyone can see me," Cecile protested, but she pulled off her hair band and put it back on, sweeping her unruly hair off her forehead. For now, she thought, looking at the back of her mother's sleek head. She'd like to see her mother or Natalie tame hair as wild as hers. Them, with their straight hair that did whatever they wanted it to.

Oh, why couldn't they get there? Cecile rubbed her thigh to soothe the sting as she looked at the land that was flattening out around them. The stunted trees were bleached white, their profiles worn short by the wind. The pale blue sky looked taut and flat all the way to the horizon, like a sheet stretched tight to cover the corners of a bed.

Lucy stuck her wet, wrinkled thumb back into her mouth and curled her finger over the bridge of her nose. She sucked contentedly for a while until her eyelids slowly drifted closed again and her thumb slid wetly from the corner of her mouth. Her head rested damp and heavy against Cecile's arm.

"Pow, pow, pow," Jack said softly. He moved the plastic army men on his lap in a silent reenactment of advance and retreat. He made the kneeling soldier holding a rifle leap up onto the car door, said, "pow-powpow" again under his breath, and sent the tall soldier with the tin cap somersaulting off his knee onto the floor.

"How're you doing, Jack?" their mother asked.

"Okay." Jack kept his eyes on the pitched battle. He hated it when people fussed at him. At eight, he had the calm, grave demeanor of a person much older. Their father had nicknamed him "the Judge."

It meant that if Jack didn't think something was good, it probably wasn't. The children all agreed it was a good name for him.

"We're almost there," Cecile told him.

"I already know that," said Jack.

Then, miraculously, the way it seemed to happen every year at the exact moment when Cecile felt she couldn't last another second, the monotonous highway ended; three speeding lanes became one. Like carnival bumper cars when the power's turned off, the cars slowed to a sedate crawl, calmly waiting their turn to merge onto the one narrow lane that signaled the end of the trip.

"It's about time," Natalie said. She promptly rolled down her window and stuck her face into the wind, her hair flying out behind her like the ears of a dog. Cecile grabbed the back of the front seat and pulled herself forward. Lucy fell sideways onto the seat, gave a startled squeak, and sat up. Her sweaty cheek was creased with sleep lines.

"There's the Lobster Hut," Jack called as they drove past a two-storied gray clapboard building that ran along a canal, with its row of bright nautical flags flapping cheerfully on its deck as if waving hello.

"Our road is next," Cecile announced.

This was the part of the trip she loved the most: when her father turned left onto Shore Road, separating their car from all the other cars that still had miles to crawl along the crowded highway to reach houses and motels scattered along the lanes that branched off to either side of the highway. Roads leading to the right meant the ocean, to the left meant the Sound.

Every year, Cecile imagined how their station wagon must look to the children in the other cars who had so much farther to go. How envious they must feel to see the lucky Thompsons, who'd be on the dock with their feet in the water before they even reached their destination. She could have been a famous person in a limousine for how it made her feel.

"Are we at Granddad's island yet?" Lucy asked sleepily.

"Not quite, sweetie." Their mother reached back

to wipe Lucy's curly, damp hair off her forehead. Lucy rested her hot cheek against her mother's hand. "Almost," her mother said.

"It's not Granddad's island," said Cecile.

"It might as well be his." Natalie pulled her head back in to add her two cents. "He has the biggest house."

"He doesn't own the whole island," Cecile said.

"Who cares? Everyone thinks it's his," Natalie said, rolling her window up as if suddenly aware of the potential effects of her impulsive behavior on her appearance. Frowning, she gathered her hair in one hand and pulled a few stray ends out of the corner of her mouth as she secured it with a clip.

But Cecile was scrupulously honest. "It's not," she said firmly.

"He could afford to buy it easily, couldn't he, Mom?" Natalie said. "He's rich enough."

"Natalie, please." Their mother hated it when they used the word rich. She said it was common.

"He could," Natalie mouthed to Cecile.

"He doesn't," Cecile mouthed back.

"The total distance from the highway to the bridge is five point two miles," Jack said. "I clocked it last year."

"Yuck," Natalie said in a superior voice as she looked out the window. "Even more of those ugly houses than last year."

They were sailing past a development, its clusters of houses spreading slowly across the flat potato fields, more destructive than locusts. Then, as surely as if they'd passed through an invisible gate, the landscape changed. Messy civilization was left behind as the car rounded a long lazy curve and burst into a clearing.

The vastness of the sky was dazzling; the white-capped bay spread out beneath it as sparkly and welcoming as a smile. The road was level with the water now; wild beach-plum bushes separated it from the bay. Golf carts and golfers dotted the smooth green to the left, but only Mr. Thompson saw. The rest of them had their eyes trained on the Island.

It rose gently out of the water like the back of a turtle floating peaceful and serene. Cecile saw the railings on the bridge over the inlet and the flag at the top of the tall white pole in front of Granddad's house. It hung limp above the trees.

"We're here!" she cried as her father slowed the car and turned onto the crushed-shell driveway. "We're here!"

"Dad!" Jack shouted, frantically stuffing his little men into their plastic bag. "Stop! You have to stop here."

"I thought maybe you were too old this year," their father teased, but he braked to a stop before the bridge so Jack could jump out, with Lucy close behind him. Cecile was about to follow when she saw Natalie hesitate. To leap out would be childish, according to her new standards. It would be far more mature to stay in the car.

If Natalie rode over the bridge, it would ruin everything.

Then Jack called, "Look! A crayfish!" and Natalie slammed her door the same time as Cecile slammed hers. They ran to the railing and hung over it, side by side, peering into the water below.

"Somebody take Lucy's hand!" their mother called as the car continued slowly up the drive, but the new order was already asserting itself. None of them paid attention.

"If she falls in, we'll fish her out," said Jack. "Look."

Lucy squatted down and crammed her face against the slats. Cecile and Natalie lifted their feet off the bridge and balanced on the railing like human seesaws as clumps of seaweed and reeds and bits of grass flew out from under them, heading for the bay on the swiftly moving tide.

"The tide's going out," Cecile announced.

"The hermit crabs will be out at the dock," said Natalie.

Their eyes met. The shared memory of scrambling on wet sand around the pilings at the dock while tiny crabs scurried for the safety of their holes passed between them. Cecile was the first to push back off the railing.

"I claim the red bucket," she said, picking up her pace.

"Blue bucket," said Natalie, moving ahead.

"I'll use the net," called Jack.

"Come on, Lucy!" the three older children shouted together. And then they were running, hair flying and legs churning as they raced past the low scrub that covered the Island, past the road that went off to the right, to the caretaker's cottage, and around the corner until they saw their grandfather's house with the deep front porch and the circular driveway with the rose bushes and their car parked in the shade under the porte cochere.

The trunk was open. Their father's arms were full of suitcases; more were piled behind the car. But still they ran. Even when Sheba came out onto the porch in her pale gray uniform and they could hear their grandfather's deep voice calling to them, they ran.

"We're going to the dock!" one of them shouted. It could have been all of them, it sounded so full. And nobody yelled, "Come back."

Chapter Two

"So! The Heathens have arrived!" King Herbert called in a booming voice as he and Sis came out onto the terrace that night. He raised the huge bottle he was carrying above his head and announced, "Let the summer games begin!"

"That's a magnum," Natalie whispered authoritatively as she and Cecile dutifully stood up.

"What's a magnum?"

"The size of the bottle. It's champagne." Natalie smoothed her hair and put her shoulders back, her eyes on King. "Mom let Harry have a glass last year. She'd better let me have one tonight."

"Me, too," Cecile said; anticipating the stinging taste of it, she made a face. Her father had given her a sip of champagne from his glass last Christmas. It tasted sour and sharp; the bubbles had tickled Cecile's nose and made her sneeze. When she hotly accused him of adding vinegar to it, on purpose so she wouldn't like it, the grown-ups around the table had roared with laughter.

Jack grabbed Lucy's hand and pulled her over to stand next to Cecile and Natalie, forming a straggly line. They would stand there, shifting their weight from one foot to the other and grinning, for as long as it took: troops, ready for inspection. The first night of cocktails on the terrace with King and Sis was a summer tradition. The month of August couldn't start without it.

"King," Mr. Thompson called from the bar under the awning, "what can I get for you?"

"What you always get for me, Andrew," said King. He strode toward their father with his hand outstretched, while their mother and Sis met near the door. They leaned toward each other and quickly touched cheeks twice, once on each side, the pearls Sis wore, even in a bathing suit, dangling between them. Cheek kisses, Cecile and Natalie used to call them, and practice as they rolled, giggling, on their bedroom floor.

Where King was big and blustery, Sis was small and dry. Her thin arms and legs looked bloodless; her pale hair was pulled back so tightly in a bun, it looked as if it must hurt. She wiggled her fingers at the children, lined up and expectant. It was the closest she would come; they gazed coolly back. Mrs. Thompson said something and the two women went to join the men at the bar, Sis swaying slightly as she clutched their mother's arm.

Natalie and Cecile exchanged quick looks.

King and Sis were the brother and sister who lived in the Pump House near the dock and had grown up with Mrs. Thompson. Sheba told them that King's wife had run off with Sis's husband, but the children were far more interested to think King might be a *real* king. For years, they felt a frisson of excitement whenever he came down to the dock or they came across him standing on the drive. "There's the king," one of them would whisper. They longed to catch him wearing his crown but never did.

It was Natalie who'd finally discovered the truth.

"He's called King because he's a Protestant," she explained one day as they gathered around her in one of their bedrooms. "Protestants give their children names like that."

"What's a Protestant?" asked Jack, who was three.

"The opposite of a Catholic," Harry said.

"Do Catholics use names like that?" said Cecile.

"Of course not," Natalie said. "Can you imagine calling Jack or Harry *King*?"

King was bigger than life; they all adored him. He was teasing their mother unmercifully now as they clustered around the bar. She slapped his arm and laughed up at him, playful and happy. Not like that day last summer, Cecile suddenly thought, when King had made her mother so angry.

He'd shown up at the house on the first morning of their vacation in a new navy blue convertible and said, "Watch this." Waving his hand like a magician, he leaned into the car and jauntily pushed a button on the dashboard. At once, the top rose majestically up from the windshield and started back, revealing a shiny new dashboard and pristine white leather seats before folding itself neatly into pleats that sank behind the backseat.

Cecile and Natalie had looked at each other, wide-eyed; they'd all been struck dumb. To ride without a top! Their parents would never dream of owning a car filled with such potential disaster. Their mother immediately launched into a story about a woman who'd had her head cut off when she ran into a truck while driving a convertible.

It had made them want to ride in it even more.

Then, wonder of wonders, King had invited them to the fair in Southampton.

"For God's sake, King," their mother said. "What do you think I've been talking about, you clod?"

"What on earth do you think is going to happen, Anne?" he protested. "I know how to drive. You make me sound like a hardened criminal."

"Please, Mom?" said Natalie.

"I'll make sure no one stands up," Harry promised.

None of them dreamed their mother would say yes, but she did; they scrambled to grab seats before she could change her mind. The front was willingly given up to Harry; the others squished into the back without bickering. None of them dared to start an argument.

"Make sure they stay seated, and don't let them put their hands outside the car. Cecile and Natalie, there's to be no fooling around in back, do you understand?" Their mother directed her glare at each of them in turn. "Jack, you listen to Harry. Harry, I'm expecting you to set an example. And King!" she cried as he started slowly off. "Make sure you put up the top while you're parked, or they'll all scald their legs when they get back."

At the fair, King brought them towering puffs of pink cotton candy on paper cones and boiled hot dogs on soft rolls and let them ride on the Ferris wheel for what felt like hours, handing more tickets to the ticket taker whenever the wheel slowed to a stop. No one threw up and no one complained and when King allowed them each to have their own large lemonade without having to share, they felt as if they were in heaven.

On the way home, King told them to "hang on to your hats" and drove very fast along Dune Road, letting them hang out over the sides of the car and scream into the wind. They came onto the Island like that, having lost all caution. Harry was standing up and shouting, waving his hat in the air at the gulls soaring above their heads, as the car clattered over the slats on the bridge, announcing their arrival.

The fury on their mother's face when they pulled in front of the house quieted them down like water dumped on flames. The children slunk guiltily out of the car while she yelled at King right in front of them, but even that couldn't destroy the wonderful day. King hung his head and looked sorry, but when their mother finally turned and stormed back into the house, letting the screen door slam behind her, King did something Cecile would never forget.

"Good day, huh, Heathens?" he said with a grin, and winked.

He had the same look of mischief on his face now as their mother pulled him over to where they stood patiently waiting. "For heaven's sake, King," she said, "look at my poor children, standing at attention. I don't know how you do it. They never behave as well for me."

"That's because you don't know how to treat them," King said. "I'm amazed they gave a brat like you a license to have them. But wait!" He stopped, opening his eyes and mouth wide, as if shocked. "People don't need a license to have children in this country, do they? It's easier to have children than it is to drive a car."

"Did you hear that?" Lucy's eyes were huge. "King called Mommy a brat."

"That's because Mommy is a brat," said Natalie.

"See what you're doing, you beast?" cried Mrs. Thompson, jabbing King in the stomach. He grabbed her hand and twisted away, but she jabbed him again, laughing. King was laughing, too. So much poking and jabbing, Cecile thought. Like children. "You're teaching my children to disrespect me, King," their mother said at last, stomping her pretty foot. "I won't have it."

"All right, all right." Clicking his heels together, King came to attention and said gruffly, "Natalie, behave yourself."

".Me?" Natalie cried, delighted.

Cecile waited for King to launch into the speech he always delivered the first night, when he declared that this was going to be the summer he would finally "teach them how to speak proper English and instill in them the manners your mother obviously hasn't." To which their mother always said, "Take them with my blessings, King, and good luck to you."

This time he didn't. After taking a hard look at them, he said, "What? Where's young Harry? Missing in action?"

Cecile and Natalie cut their eyes at each other.

"Dad got him a job at one of his paper mills in Canada," their mother said. "He was sixteen in December, you know."

"Canada?" King's thick eyebrows rose up like wings above his dark eyes. "Going to make a man out of the prodigal son this summer, is that it?"

"He's hardly cutting down trees," their mother

said coolly. "Dad got him a job washing dishes."

"Washing dishes!" King laughed and slapped his leg. "No more lazing around on the golf course, earning big tips as a caddy, hey? You're going to toughen him up washing dishes."

"You'll have to talk to Andrew about that." Their mother's voice was tight. "It was his idea."

"Oh. I see." King and she looked at each other for an instant, and then King gave a curt nod. "Right," he said, twirling around to face the children again. "Enough frivolity now." He took a brisk step to the left and stuck out his hand. "Jack, good to see you, sir. Are you and I going after those porgies again this year?"

"Yes, sir!" Jack said, jerking King's hand up and down twice.

"Good man."

King stepped in front of Cecile. "Cecile Thompson, you're looking spry this summer." Cecile beckoned for him to come closer when they shook hands. "Can we go to the fair again?" she whispered into his ear.

King glanced over his shoulder at her mother. "Only if I can smuggle you all out in burlap bags," he whispered back. "I'll pretend you're potatoes."

Natalie was next.

"My, my," King said as he took her hand. He sounded surprised. "If you don't look remarkably like your mother at this age, young Natalie," he said, bowing his head ever so slightly.

It gave Cecile the strangest empty feeling in her chest to see Natalie blush. How long had Natalie known? Because she did know. Cecile could see it in the way Natalie lifted her chin to meet King's gaze. The knowledge was in Natalie's imperious profile, too, so like their mother's. In the curve of her smile.

Their mother was beautiful; they both thought so. One night, years ago, when Cecile and Natalie had huddled in their nightgowns at the top of the stairs to spy on a dinner party, their great-aunt Agatha, who was very old and beautiful herself, had snuck them up some ice cream. She sat on the top step with them while they ate, her diamond earrings and necklace glittering in the dark like stars. When their mother appeared in the front hall below, dazzling in a scarlet gown with rhinestone straps, Great-Aunt Agatha had told the awed little girls that the conversation used to stop when their mother was young and she entered the room.

Cecile had instantly felt the thrill of it: the hushed voices, the admiring faces. She'd longed to be beautiful from that moment on. Having King acknowledge that Natalie was felt like the end of a dream. Because King was right. Even though their mother's hair was dark and Natalie's light, they had the same ivory skin, dark eyes, sculpted mouths. Cecile hadn't realized it until now, but Natalie and her mother had both known. The look they exchanged was like the password to a club to which Cecile would never belong.

"Are you torturing my family over here, King?" Mr. Thompson said as he and Sis joined them, drinks in hand.

"Only your wife, Andrew," said King.

"She might say I do quite a bit of that," Mr. Thompson said.

"King has been torturing your wife all his life," Sis said drily. "It's his favorite pastime."

"Yes, but when King does it, she doesn't mind. Drink, darling?"

"Thanks." Mrs. Thompson took the glass he held out to her without looking at him as she slipped her arm through King's. "It's time for Jack and Lucy to get ready for bed. Run and find Sheba, you two," she said. "And Natalie and Cecile? No dock tonight. It's been a long day."

"Troops dismissed," said King.

"Mom's awfully buddy-buddy with King," Cecile said as she followed Natalie into the living room.

"They grew up together," Natalie said, shrugging. "Besides, Mom's giving Dad the business."

"Because of Harry?"

"I don't blame him for not wanting Harry around. 'My handsome son this.' 'My handsome son that.'" Natalie tossed her hair. "I'm sick of it, too."

"You're making that up, Natalie," Cecile said in a fierce whisper. "Dad doesn't feel that way."

"That's how much you know." Natalie stopped in

front of the mirror above the table in the front hall. "Don't worry, when she gets what she wants, she'll go back to being sweetness and light again."

"But she can't have Harry," Cecile insisted. "He's in Canada."

"She has her ways. . . ." Natalie's voice drifted off; she looked at her reflection intently. Lifting her chin, she allowed a hint of a smile, as if posing for a portrait. "King's so full of it, saying that I look like Mom, don't you think?" she asked, raising false eyes to meet Cecile's in the mirror. "I thought it would never end," Natalie said, but her eyes were bright, her color still high.

Chapter Three

Cecile was the first one awake. She stretched her arms over her head and reached with her toes for the bottom of the bed. It's only our third day, she thought contentedly, letting her muscles go slack. We have twenty-eight more to go. When she couldn't remember how many days she'd been here and didn't know how many days were left, *then* she'd be on vacation.

She lay on her back in the cool, dim room at the end of the hall that she shared with Natalie and Lucy and watched the gauze curtains on the window behind Lucy's bed ripple over Lucy's sleeping body. Lucy was on her stomach; her tangled curls covered her face. She had kicked off her sheets. Her short pajama top was wrapped around her chest, her skinny brown legs flailed out to either side as though she were a rag doll, tossed.

Natalie had snuggled so far under her white cotton blanket that the only sign of her was her blond hair splayed across the pillow. The blue-and-white canopy bed she claimed would be hers when she got married, because she was the oldest girl, had belonged to their grandmother. Cecile was glad to let Natalie sleep it in; it felt like a dead person's bed. She pretended to be grudging when she let Natalie claim it every year, but secretly, she was glad. It meant Natalie owed her.

Natalie was dead to the world. Already she'd fallen back into her languid, bored fourteen-year-old self. She wouldn't wake up until after nine, when she'd drift down to the terrace in her nightgown to eat breakfast, holding out her pinky as she sipped orange juice.

"You are so twelve," she'd said yesterday morning when Cecile came running back from the dock in her bathing suit to grab a muffin. "You haven't even combed your hair."

"You are so a hundred million," Cecile shot back. She'd already spotted three horseshoe crabs in the shallow water under the dock by then, and netted a slew of clear jellyfish that she piled on the float before gently slipping them back into the water so they wouldn't die. It made her wild to think of wasting time the way Natalie did.

She would never be as old as that, Cecile vowed. It was horrible the way getting old made people put on such airs. Natalie looked miserable half the time. She heard the faint click of the door to the terrace below their room, and the almost imperceptible rumble of her father's voice. Then her mother's clipped response.

Cecile kicked off the sheet and slipped her legs over the edge of the bed. If she didn't hurry, Lucy would wake up and cry, "Wait for me!" Pulling off her nightgown, she dropped it on the ottoman where yesterday's T-shirt lay in a crumpled heap. She slid that over her head and stepped into her shorts lying on the floor, pulling them up over the underwear she hadn't taken off last night.

It was one of their mother's rules that they should never go to sleep wearing the day's underwear. Rules about my own underwear, Cecile thought. Ridiculous. She hardly wore underwear on the Island anyway, she spent so much time in a bathing suit. She didn't brush her hair a hundred strokes both morning and night, either, or brush her teeth for as long as it took the white sand to run out in the tiny hourglass her mother put on the glass shelf above the sink.

Cecile ran on tiptoe down the upstairs hallway, skimming her hand over the smooth banister as she flew down the curving stairs. The dark floor of the front hall was cool on the soles of her feet; the hall felt dim and still, like a cave. Someone had opened the front door; the driveway was brilliant in the morning sun. Cecile pressed her face against the screen and breathed in, testing for the warm metallic smell the screen would have later in the day. All she could smell now was the faint perfume of the roses in the vase on the table behind her.

A pot clanking against the stove meant Sheba was

in the kitchen, making breakfast. Any minute now, she'd push through the swinging door with a tray laden with a pot of coffee and glasses of freshly squeezed orange juice. Cecile had to fly if she was going to get out of the house without anyone seeing her.

She slipped out the screen door and ran toward the dock, her heart racing triumphantly for having so narrowly escaped capture. It was wonderful, not having to sit down to breakfast the way they did at home. Eggs, cereal, milk, toast, use your napkin, please . . . it was enough to make her scream. On the Island, Harry and she and Natalie used to pretend they were prisoners escaping from jail when they snuck out of the house every morning. Yet another game Natalie now called babyish.

Who gives a care? Cecile's heart sang. The crushed shells mixed with the gravel on the drive were sharp beneath her feet.

The smell of salt and marsh hung heavy in the air: The tide was out. Hermit crabs by the dozens, so densely packed they looked like a magic carpet, would be moving around the pilings. That is, until Cecile set one foot on the sand and then they'd be gone—*whoosh!*—scuttling sideways with a speed that never failed to amaze her, each crab disappearing down a hole. Then the beach would be empty except for the squiggly piles of wet sand, evidence of their hard labor.

Cecile ran down the wooden stairs to the wide deck that separated the dock from the drive. The changing cabanas stood empty and expectant on one side. The boathouse on the other smelled of salt and creosote. Someone was standing on the float at the far end of the dock. Cecile halted, disappointed not to be the first.

But wait. It was only Jack, with a green life vest over his pajamas, fishing; he didn't count. She ran past the empty berths, past Mr. Peabody's dinghy tied to a ladder with its rope hanging slack, until she came to the top of the short ramp to the swimming float, where she asked, "Does Mom know you're down here?" in a big-sister voice.

Children weren't allowed on the dock by themselves

until they were ten and had passed Granddad's rigid swimming test. It was the one Island rule no one was allowed to break. Disobedience meant being banned from the dock area for a week, a punishment worse than death.

"It's all right. He's with me!" Cecile twirled around to see King coming out of the boathouse with an armload of life jackets and start toward them. "Good morning, Miss Thompson," he said when he reached her. He gave a courtly bow.

"Morning."

King dumped the jackets on a bench and took off his cap. Smoothing his dark hair back from his forehead, he turned slowly in a circle without speaking, gazing at the scene around them as if he were alone. Cecile took it in, too: the tall wall of marsh grass that hid the complex maze of winding channels that boats took in and out on their way from the bay to the dock. The long roofline of the clubhouse etched cleanly on the horizon on the point to the right.

Behind them, the flag on the shiny white pole that would flap and strain, clinking its metal rope against the wood when the wind picked up later in the day, hung limp, as if still asleep. Cecile squinted up at King from time to time, patient. He never bothered with them much when the other adults weren't around. He was the relaxing kind of grown-up who'd never had children of his own, so he didn't have the annoying habit parents had of warning their children against actions they'd never dream of taking, or telling them what to do when they already had plans of their own.

"Why would I tell her not to fall in the water?" King asked her mother one day when Mrs. Thompson came down to the dock and found Cecile, then six, standing with her toes hanging over the edge of the dock at the deep end, watching King ready his boat. "The child's got a brain. She knows she shouldn't fall in."

Cecile had swelled with pride, hearing him say she had a brain. "I have a brain, you know," she'd say after that whenever anyone in her family told her what to do. She stood beside him now, biding her time until he was through with his inspection so she could ask him a question. King finally put his hat back on, squaring it on his forehead, just so. "As I told Jack," he said to her as if their conversation hadn't been interrupted, "I'll only be down here for another ten minutes. I'm playing golf with your father."

"He's eating breakfast," Cecile said.

"Is he? I'd better hurry then." King started back up the dock.

"Where's the *Rammer*?" Cecile called.

"I don't expect her until tomorrow evening," King answered. "Ten minutes, heathens." He disappeared inside the boathouse.

Cecile walked down the ramp and sat on the edge of the float at a safe distance from Jack's fishing line. She adored King's boat. He took the whole family, including Granddad, out on it for a whole day every summer. If it wasn't at the dock, it meant King had rented it again. People were willing to pay him huge sums of money, he said, to travel in it up and down the coast from Maine to Florida.

"Did he say anything about taking us out for a ride?" she asked Jack.

Jack shook his head.

"Did you ask him?"

"No."

"He'll take us." Cecile swung her feet back and forth in the water. The tide was sweeping the night's refuse from the inlet out to the bay. Clumps of seaweed, patches of dirty foam, broken reeds; the swift, dark water swirled around the pilings, momentarily thwarted, and then moved on again, its glossy surface broken now and then by a fish coming up for food.

"Look, Jack!" Cecile cried. She pointed to a small circle on the water's surface halfway between the dock and the edge of the marsh grass. It grew larger and larger as she watched.

"I saw it," said Jack. "They're all over the place."

Seagulls landed on pilings and laughed their mocking, human laughs; boats started up their engines in the distance; water lapped against the dock. The only way you could tell the passing of time was by the sun. Cecile felt it on her back now, warmer than before. The kind of warm that would soon be hot.

After a while, she heard a high, excited voice and the light patter of feet on the dock as Lucy ran toward them. "Be careful," their mother called. Cecile looked up to see her stop at the door to the boathouse, leaving Lucy to run the rest of the way by herself. Lucy stopped when she came to the top of the ramp and, clutching her bucket and shovel tightly in one hand, grasped the railing with the other. She walked carefully down to the float, keeping her eyes on her feet, the way she'd been taught.

Lucy's yellow bathing suit was covered with pink flamingos and had bows on either hip; her white cotton hat with the frilly rim was already sliding off the back of her head. "I had blueberry pancakes," she announced as she squatted down next to Jack's pail to watch three small minnows that hung, suspended, at the bottom. When Lucy stuck in her shovel, they darted frantically around the edges, as if swimming for their lives.

"Lucy, don't," said Jack.

Lucy pulled her shovel out but remained squatting. Their mother had worked her way lazily toward them and stopped at the top of the ramp. She leaned against a piling.

"It's going to be hot," she said as she lifted a hand to shield her eyes. In her pale blue linen shorts and matching sleeveless blouse, with her dark hair held back by a blue ribbon, it really could have been Natalie standing there; she looked that young.

"Did King say which day we're going on the *Rammer*?" Cecile asked.

"We didn't talk about it." Her mother smiled absently down at her. "Have you had breakfast yet?"

"I'm not hungry," Jack said.

"I haven't." The minute she said it, Cecile was starving.

"Come on, you three." Their mother turned and started back. "Bring Lucy, would you, Cecile?"

"I want to stay!" Lucy wailed, but Cecile scooped her up around the stomach, cutting her off in mid-cry, and carried her up the ramp, oblivious to her indignant yells and kicking feet. Lucy struck out with her shovel when Cecile finally dumped her on the dock, but Cecile was too quick.

"Last one up is a rotten egg!" she cried. She took the stairs two at a time and ran onto the drive. Only when she could no longer hear Lucy's wails did she slow to a walk. The air was heavy with privet. The Pump House turret rose behind the tall hedge on her left like something out of a fairy tale. Cecile plucked a blade of grass from the side of the drive and held the palms of her hands tightly together, stretching the blade taut between her thumbs. She blew a sharp blast of air on it; the sound was high and shrill, like a demented seagull.

At the sound of tires on gravel, she looked up. Their car was pulling out of Granddad's driveway. Her father and Granddad were in the front, King was in the back.

They didn't look her way. Cecile didn't call out. She was thinking about the terrace; how cool and quiet it would be now with no one on it. The newspaper would be flung down in restless sections on a chaise, the glass-top table littered with empty cups and plates, the stubs of her father's cigarettes sending up their last futile drifts of smoke from an ashtray.

And Granddad's chaise lounge—the one in its special spot in the shade under the awning in the far corner of the terrace that the children knew to leap up and out of whenever he appeared—would be empty. She could stop in the kitchen and get something to eat, and then lie in wait for Natalie to appear in her nightgown, and see her, Cecile, on the throne. Anticipating that moment, and the expression on Natalie's face, Cecile ran.

Chapter Four

All the long drive back from the ocean the next day, the crotch of Cecile's bathing suit was heavy against her, filled with the sand she had collected while riding the waves. The skin on her face felt scratchy and dry.

Lucy had insisted on keeping her beach ball clutched to her chest as she got into the backseat. It had dropped small clumps of wet sand that scratched Cecile's thighs. Cecile wiped it off but more sand appeared. She had given up.

"It hurts to breathe," Cecile said. She rested her head against the back of the seat and closed her eyes. She took quick, shallow breaths to avoid feeling the tightness in her chest.

"You're waterlogged," her mother said from

behind the steering wheel. "I told you to come out earlier."

"I'm waterlogged, too," said Lucy. She had dug holes on the shore all day and run back up the beach, shrieking, as the rising tide filled them in. No water had touched her body higher than her knobby knees. Her suit was dry.

"You didn't even swim," Natalie said.

"I did too," said Lucy. "Didn't I, Jack?"

"I saw her," Jack said to keep the peace. Jack was always the one to keep the peace.

"Then why is your suit dry?" Natalie said, and reached quickly over Cecile's lap to run her finger meanly under the rim of Lucy's suit where it circled her thigh.

"Natalie, please." Their mother sighed when Lucy started to cry.

"Oh, all right, you baby," said Natalie. "You swam."

Lucy stuck her thumb in her mouth and quieted down. It was an aimless kind of bickering. They were all used to it. They rode in exhausted silence until they reached the bridge. When Cecile finally heard the familiar sound of the tires on wood, she took a deep breath. The tightness was gone.

"Everyone in the shower," their mother ordered when the car stopped in front of the house. "Don't go into the house empty-handed!" she cried as the doors flew open. "Towel on the line, Jack!"

The first touch of the shower's cool water on her hot skin made Cecile flinch. She looked down at the bathing suit imprinted on her body. Her first sunburn of the summer reminded her of the outfits she put on her paper dolls with tabs. The imprint of her bathing suit was startling against her red arms and legs, the lines between red and white as straight and clean as if drawn with a ruler. Turning slightly, she saw the straps running up over her shoulders, the scoop of its neck tracing a graceful curve on her chest. Oh, but it was going to sting in the middle of the night. She could already feel it.

She held her face under the stream of water. She washed her hair. Stepping out of the tub, she wrapped a thick towel around her body and tiptoed down the hall to her parents' room. Lucy's high-pitched voice rose above the running water in the master bathroom. Her mother was giving Lucy a bath in her huge tub with lots of bubbles. The air smelled of strawberries.

If she'd been nine, or even ten, she would have gone into the bathroom to show Lucy and her mother the red paper doll wearing a white bathing suit. Instead, Cecile stood in front of the full-length mirror and let her towel slip to the floor. She turned around and craned her head to look at her back. The suit was perfect there, as well.

Walking across the soft carpet to her mother's makeup table, she gazed at the array of pale green boxes, dark red lipstick tubes, and exotic jars in different shapes and sizes. Her mother's moisturizer was in the dark pink jar. Cecile picked it up. Their mother had laughingly dabbed tiny drops of it on their noses and cheeks when Cecile and Natalie were little and wanted to know what it felt like. It even smelled expensive.

Cecile checked guiltily over her shoulder and then quickly poured a bit of the cool liquid into the palm of her hand. Slowly she spread it over her face and neck. How luxurious and smooth it was! She poured more and recklessly slathered it over her chest and down her stomach. Her hand sliding across her skin felt sophisticated and daring.

The front door banged; deep male voices sounded in the front hall. Feeling as exposed as if she were standing naked on an empty stage when the curtain unexpectantly rose, Cecile dashed back across the room and wrapped the towel tightly around her. She rubbed her face vigorously with both hands. When the door opened, she turned toward it, innocent and welcoming.

"Oh. I thought it was your mother." Her father strode across the room to his dresser. His tanned forearms looked muscular and strong; his dark hair was firmly slicked back, there wasn't a strand out of place. "Did you have fun at the beach?" he asked as he took a fistful of change out of his pants pocket and dropped it into a silver dish.

"It was great." Cecile inched her way toward the door. "Did you and Granddad win your game?"

"We did, no thanks to me. I had a rotten day. Four over par." Her father undid the clasp on his heavy watch and dropped it on the dresser next to the dish. "Where's your mother?" he said.

"In the bathroom with Lucy."

He gave Cecile a quick, appraising glance. "Looks like someone got a lot of sun."

"I did."

"Andrew! Is that Cecile I hear with you?"

When her father opened the bathroom door, Cecile reluctantly went and stood beside him. The air in the bathroom was steamy and thick. Mrs. Thompson was kneeling by the side of the tub with Lucy in front of her. Lucy had a paper-doll bathing suit, too, but her arms and legs were brown. She had both hands on her mother's shoulders to steady herself as she stepped carefully into the white underpants her mother was holding open.

"I thought I heard you two," Mrs. Thompson said. "How was your game?"

"Your father saved my hide."

"You've saved his often enough."

Their formal voices were almost as bad as their silence. How dare they keep this up? Cecile was in an agony to get away.

"You're just the person I wanted to see, Cecile," her mother said.

"She was admiring herself in front of the mirror," said Mr. Thompson.

"I was not!" Cecile wrapped her towel more tightly around her. Why hadn't she worn her robe? "I was looking for Mom," she said. "I don't do silly things like that."

"Methinks the lady doth protest too much." Her father reached out to ruffle her hair, but Cecile stepped skittishly back. "Don't," she said in a low voice. She felt she would cry if he touched her. She hated him.

"Leave her alone, Andrew," her mother said.

"I was teasing her, for God's sake. Am I not allowed to tease my daughter, either? Is that part of my sentence?"

"I guess it is." Her mother flashed him a brittle smile.

They looked at each other the way only the two of them could—it felt almost like hate. Cecile's stomach churned. Their silence bore down on her shoulders; her neck ached.

Her father abruptly spun on his heels and walked toward the closet. "Then I guess you're not interested in the message King asked me to give you," he said to Cecile as he opened the door.

Why punish her? It was so unfair. "What?" Cecile cried. "What did he say?"

"The *Rammer*'s coming in. King said you'd been asking."

Cecile could have melted onto the carpet with relief. Escape!

"Great! Thanks!" she said, and headed for the door.

"Cecile, wait!" her mother called. "Take Lucy with you."

"But it's coming in now," Cecile wailed. "Lucy's too slow!"

"Take me! Take me!" Lucy cried from the bathroom.

"Mom . . ."

"You heard your mother." Her father sat on the edge of their bed and crossed one leg over his knee. He leaned down to untie his shoe. "What's the big rush? You've seen it come in a million times."

I just want to *go*, Cecile wanted to cry. I don't want to *wait*.

But Lucy was keeping up her lament in the bathroom. Cecile never should have come in here in the first place. "Oh, all right," she said ungraciously, "but make her hurry."

The *Rammer* was berthed by the time she reached the dock. Cecile trailed behind as Lucy ran eagerly down the steps. The *Rammer* sat massive and important, its hosed decks gleaming in the late afternoon sun. Ropes had been neatly coiled, fishing poles put away.

Her mother had told Cecile to keep Lucy out of the water. She walked along the edge of the sand behind Lucy now, watching the cabin cruiser as it rocked rhythmically against the pilings. She felt empty and clean; she thought she'd drift up into the sky like a balloon if it weren't for the heavy, contented tiredness in her arms and legs to hold her down. Her footprints shimmered with life for a second before they melted back into the sand. Tiny waves lapped soothingly at the sunburned tops of her feet.

There was a shout of laughter from the *Rammer*'s deck. Cecile saw a tall, white-haired man sitting in a deck chair under the awning. He smiled broadly at something another man was saying, then leaned back contentedly and gave another shout of laughter. Suddenly, as if on an invisible lift, a boy rose smoothly from the cabin below and came onto the deck carrying a tray. He handed a tall glass to the laughing man and a shorter glass to the other man. He placed a small bowl on the table between them.

A shiver of excitement ran the length of Cecile's body.

The boy was a crew member. She could tell by the easy way he stood moving with the rocking of the boat, the tray dangling at his side as he waited to execute any other requests the two men might make.

He was tan and thin; his dark hair reached almost to his shoulders. Calf muscles stood out on his long legs; his khaki shorts hung from his hips.

He had to be about Harry's age. Harry wore his shorts like that, too. Maybe he played soccer like Harry; he looked strong. It was strange, how seeing a boy her own brother's age should make her feel so excited, so oddly out of breath. Something fluttered nervously in the pit of her stomach. She felt herself staring.

"Lucy," she cried, shaking herself out of her trance. "Come here! Hurry!"

Cecile looked frantically for something— anything—to capture her sister's attention as Lucy ran toward her with tiny steps, as quick and eager as a tern.

Cecile grabbed Lucy's net and, brittle and self-conscious as a starlet, pranced along the edge of the water sending up a spray of sunlit droplets, like something out of a movie. Not knowing why she did so, she hunted crabs more eagerly, cried out over each one more loudly. She held her net, heavy with catch, higher in the air so that anyone on the *Rammer* might see and be curious.

Crouching to empty her booty into Lucy's bucket, she wondered what she might look like to someone on the boat. Oh, why wasn't her skin less pink, why didn't her hair lie more smoothly on her head? She was painfully aware of the boy as she stood up.

Maybe she would appear older with Lucy at her side, Cecile thought, and tried to take Lucy's hand. But Lucy would have none of it.

"Nonononono!" Lucy cried, twisting and turning like a fish on a line. Cecile dropped her hand.

"All right!" she whispered. "Be quiet."

When the slatted doors on the cabanas slammed shut, Cecile spun around. Two women came out with their skin glistening, their hair sleek. They had to be with the men on the *Rammer*.

"I'll get us another net," Cecile said to Lucy quickly, and ran up the stairs into the boathouse. When she came back out, the women were leaning on the railing, looking at the bay. They turned to her and smiled.

"What do you hope to catch with that?" the woman with red hair asked. Even though she'd taken a shower, she looked hot. Her neck and shoulders were an angry red.

"Minnows swimming along the shore, mostly," said Cecile. Then, hurriedly, "It's for my little sister."

"Do you children live here?" the other woman asked. She was taller than the redhead, and blond. Her skin was a dark, even tan like Natalie's. Skin like that never burns, Cecile thought. Her finger went up to touch the tiny blisters on the bridge of her nose. Natalie never got blisters, either.

"Our grandfather does," she said.

"What, in the big house?"

Cecile nodded.

"Is that your brother?" The redhead nodded toward Jack, fishing on the float.

"Yes."

"How many more of you are there?"

"Two."

"My goodness," said the blonde. "Aren't you the lucky ones?"

The women moved down the dock, calling to the men to help them aboard. Cecile went back to Lucy, who was squatting down, working industriously to dig a hole even as it filled with water. "Lucy," Cecile said coaxingly, "let's go see if Jack caught anything."

"I don't want to."

"Mom said you're not supposed to get wet." Cecile grabbed Lucy's hand to pull her up and said impatiently, "Come on."

"Let me go!" Lucy shouted, planting her heels in the sand, refusing to budge.

"Fine." Cecile let go. Lucy fell back and landed on her bottom, her face registering the shock.

"Baby," Cecile said. "Serves you right."

At the sound of an outboard motor, Cecile looked up. The boy was pulling away in the dinghy that had been tied to the back of the *Rammer*. He steered it expertly out toward the sea grass in a smooth arc, sending up a bright wall of water behind him. He lifted a hand to Jack as he went past the float. Jack raised his hand back and stood watching as the dinghy disappeared.

"Go ahead, get your feet wet," Cecile said as Lucy stubbornly got to her feet and brushed at the wet circle on the back of her sundress. "See if I care." Cecile went back to the deck and sat on a bench. Leaning her arms on the railing, she stared, unseeing, at the bay.

He would have waved to her, too, if she'd been on the float. He would at least have seen her.

Natalie appeared on the stairs a few minutes later. She'd blown her hair dry and she held her head carefully so as not to disturb its smooth straightness as she came down the steps. Good thing there wasn't a breeze off the water or Natalie would go right back to the house; Cecile was dying to talk to her.

"God, Cecile," Natalie said, frowning at her fastidiously. "You look like a lobster."

Cecile felt the red of her face clash even more hideously with that of her hair under her sister's gaze. "The *Rammer*'s in," she said.

"How can you tell?" Natalie's voice was heavy with fourteen-year-old sarcasm.

"Captain Stone has a new cabin boy."

"How exciting."

Cecile should have known Natalie wouldn't care. People who worked on the *Rammer* didn't interest her; it was the women whose husbands had enough money to charter it who she'd care about. She'd study them closely for their clothes and shoes and hair.

At home, Natalie poured over the magazines their mother subscribed to: magazines filled with photographs of people on horses, mansions with turrets and gables, the weddings of strangers. There were reports about elaborate parties where women acted like children and wore costumes and masks— even feathers in their hair. The men wore navy blazers with white linen pants and loafers without socks, like a uniform. Everyone looked so much the same. Cecile couldn't understand what Natalie and her mother found so interesting.

"Mom sent me to bring you up for dinner," Natalie said, her eyes fastened on the boat. "She wants to see you before they leave."

Cecile might have protested, but now another new feeling was running through her: She didn't want

Natalie to be here when the boy came back. He wouldn't be able to miss her, with the sun glinting off her hair like that and the ends of her shirt tied in a knot, revealing her flat, tanned stomach above her shorts.

Cecile was suddenly giddy with the need for them to leave.

"Lucy! Jack! *Viens ici!*" she shouted as she leaped onto the bench and waved her arms above her head. How pretentious, calling to them in French! She sounded like Miss Mathieu, her French teacher, who refused to speak to the class in English.

You look ridiculous, she told herself; she didn't care. "*À table,*" she called as loudly as she liked. "Dinner!"

"What're you doing?" Natalie said in a furious whisper. "Get down."

Too late. The people on the *Rammer* had heard. The blond woman called out to Jack as he made his way slowly toward his sisters, holding the tip of his pole out over the railing so he could trail his bait behind him in the water.

Whatever he said made them all laugh.

"God, you are so immature." Natalie's voice was low and passionate. She turned and walked angrily up the stairs; Cecile's relief at seeing her go was immense. She sagged onto the bench; the balloon had lost its air. Suddenly she had all the time in the world.

Cecile waited patiently for Lucy to make her way across the sand and then held her bucket while Lucy rinsed her feet in the faucet next to the boathouse.

"What did they want?" she asked Jack when he came up to them.

"They wanted to know if we were from France."

"What'd you say?"

"I said we were from Connecticut."

"You dope," said Cecile, grinning. Then, with greater feeling, "You turkey!"

"They talked to me as if I was five," said Jack. He was small for his age and accustomed to being underestimated. The combination of his size and his beautiful dark eyes and hair made people dote on him in foolish ways. Cecile had seen it happen again and again. Jack's scorn was monumental.

"If Mom was here, she'd call them Nosey Parkers," he said disgustedly.

"Nosey Parkers! Nosey Parkers!" Lucy picked up the words and started to chant.

Her shrill voice carried out over the water.

"Lucy, be quiet!" Cecile and Jack said in loud whispers.

But Lucy was wild with the sound of it. She stomped her feet and marched in circles. "Nosey Parkers, Nosey Parkers!" she cried.

Cecile clamped her hand over Lucy's mouth, trying not to laugh, and carried her, struggling, up the stairs. She couldn't imagine what they looked like to the people on the *Rammer*, and she didn't care. The dinghy was still gone.

Jack ran behind her with Lucy's bucket, bent over, laughing with the joke of it.

When she knew they were out of sight of the boat, Cecile dumped Lucy unceremoniously on her feet on the driveway. Lucy immediately set up a roar.

"Onward, Nosey Parkers!" commanded Jack. He raised Lucy's net high in the air as if it were a flag.

Cecile scooped up Lucy again and carried her piggy-back, bouncing her up and down as they went and chanting, so that by the time they rounded the corner onto Granddad's drive and saw their mother standing on the front porch, waiting, Lucy was beaming.

Chapter Five

"Beep, beep! Coming through."

Jack trotted up behind Cecile as she walked slowly down to the dock the next morning, and passed her. He held a large red thermos with a metal top firmly against his chest with both arms.

"Who's that for?" Cecile said.

"Sis," Jack called without stopping. "It's her lemonade."

"I hope she gives you a tip!"

Knowing Sis, she was sitting under her umbrella at the far end of the beach, as far away from the dock as she could get. Mrs. Harris, King's and Sis's housekeeper, set Sis up there a few mornings a week. Sis stayed all morning, her huge sunglasses covering half her face, a stack of magazines on a small table next to her, a cooler at her feet. She rarely moved out from under the umbrella until after lunch, when Mrs. Harris reappeared to carry everything back up to the house with Sis teetering along behind her, empty-handed.

Now she has Jack fetching and carrying for her, too, Cecile thought. Rather him than me. She heard a car crunching along the drive behind her and turned, expecting to see Mr. Peabody, the Island caretaker, in his ancient station wagon with wooden slats, or the white delivery van from the grocer in Southampton that delivered groceries twice a week to Granddad's house, but the dark car working its way toward her was unfamiliar.

People hardly ever came onto the Island who didn't belong there; they must be lost. Cecile stepped back onto the grass and waited with a polite face to give directions.

The car slid heavily past without stopping; several pale profiles stared straight ahead inside. How rude, for people who weren't even supposed to be here, to ignore her like that. Only one round face, as pale as the moon, gazed back at her through the rear window. It was a little boy wearing a cap.

She trailed after them, watching as the car slowly came to a stop at the dock. There was a pause, and then four doors opened and five people got out: a mother, a father, and three children. Large and pale, with brown hair and prominent ears, they stood blinking uncertainly in the sudden glare like moles emerging from their tunnel. The boys wore dark pants, white shirts, and striped ties. The girl wore a white blouse with a Peter Pan collar and a plaid skirt.

Interlopers, Cecile thought scornfully; the name was instinctive and fatal. Interlopers was what the Thompson children had always called people who came onto the Island for a day or two; guests of Mrs. Miller, maybe, who had owned a small house. Or passengers on the boats that stopped at the dock to refuel. Interlopers didn't get to *stay*, they were passing through.

Whenever these strangers arrived, the Thompson children would stand as suspicious and alert as savages who watched invaders pull their boats up onto the shore, to see who they were. The minute they were identified as Interlopers, one of the children would shriek. Then they'd all start to shriek and run as fast as they could to hide under the dock or in the boathouse. If they were in the yard, they'd duck inside the huge lilac bush at the head of the drive-way, which they'd turned into a fort with towels. Huddled together, they'd clamp their hands over their mouths to keep from laughing as the Interlopers walked past.

If their mother or father were around, one of them might say, "Don't be so silly," but nobody stopped them. Crouched down, peering through branches, exhilarated by their own silliness, they could hear the Interlopers coming. Their heavy steps got closer and closer, their loud voices exclaiming over things they saw along the drive. King's turret poking above the trees, maybe, or the magnificent oak in Granddad's garden. More than once, the children heard one of them say, "Who do you think lives in that big house?"

These Interlopers who had invaded by car were

the worst; they'd glided right by, without saying hello, and stood between Cecile and the dock. Serves them right, they're hot, she thought. Look at them, in school uniforms and shoes and socks on the Island in the middle of summer. She felt their eyes on her and grew proud. She was so obviously an insider, and cool, in her navy blue tank suit with a towel flung over her shoulder.

Standing a little straighter, she walked toward them on bare feet without flinching. She tossed her head the way Natalie would have done and understood what it meant for the first time: You can come or go, my life will stay the same.

The girl was openly staring at her. She was about Cecile's age, her wide, freckled face was flushed; her pale hair hung lank and damp. She looked hot and lumpy in her crumpled blouse; one of her knee socks had given up and fallen down around her ankle. Cecile couldn't remember having been stared at with such interest before. She knew at once the girl was willing to be her friend. It made her feel aloof and powerful.

As quickly as her confidence had lifted her up, it dropped her like a wave breaking against the sand. Cecile felt the jolt as she caught the eye of the older boy. He was rocking the knot of his tie from side to side to loosen it and watching her. Could he really have run his eyes up and down her like that? How dare he! She was excruciatingly aware of her flat chest. It was all she could do to stop herself from bringing up her hands to protect it.

Because it wasn't completely flat anymore; disks, round as quarters, were pushing their way up under her skin to form small bumps. Cecile had longed to stop them from the first morning she'd noticed them. She didn't dare look to see if this Interloper could see them; he'd smirk if he could; she'd die. Oh, and her skinny legs, too. Cecile tugged at her suit.

The little boy and his parents turned away from the seawall and walked back to the car. "Wait until we get to the cottage, Leo," Cecile heard the woman say as the boy started taking off his cap. "You'll burn." Leo settled it back over his wide brow again without arguing.

The cottage. Cecile's heart sunk. They weren't lost, they were staying. The cottage was the only property on the Island that was for rent. Its owner—frail, reclusive Mrs. Miller, who had vacationed there alone for as long as Cecile could remember with her nurse and her spoiled shih tzu, Fritz—had died during the winter. In one of the frequent bits of scandalous information Sheba passed on to them when they ate in the kitchen, the children had learned that Mrs. Miller's family was squabbling over her will.

"There's nothing like money to tear a family up," is what she'd said.

"Having it, or not having it?" Natalie asked.

"Both."

Maybe the Interlopers were Mrs. Miller's grandchildren. Or maybe they were just renters. Either way, these pale strangers were going to run around their Island and fish from their dock. Cecile ducked her head and skirted around the group without saying hello, knowing she was rude. Wait until Natalie hears, she thought as she skimmed along the dock toward the float. She'll have a fit.

But Natalie didn't have a fit.

"How old are they?" she said without opening her eyes. She was lying on her back on a striped towel with the straps of her new flowered two-piece bathing suit untied. Her arms and legs glistened with baby oil. Her stomach glistened, too. Cecile stared; she hadn't seen as much of Natalie's body since they'd stopped taking baths together, years ago.

"How can you go out in that?" she'd demanded when Natalie and their mother came home from the store and Natalie modeled it for her. "It doesn't cover any more of your body than underwear."

"I suppose you're going to wear your swim-team tank suit for the rest of your life?" Natalie said as she twirled, delighted.

"Wait till you're fourteen," her mother had said with a knowing smile. "You're going to want the same thing."

"I never will," Cecile said.

She felt more determined now, seeing that a pool

of oil had collected around Natalie's belly button. She looked away.

"Are there any boys?" Natalie murmured.

"Two," Cecile said. "But they're funny looking."

"Oh?" Natalie opened her eyes and leaned up on one elbow. "How old?"

"Natalie, they're Interlopers."

"Cecile, how old?"

The betrayal of it. She should have known. As long as it was a boy, Natalie wouldn't care *what* he looked like. "Traitor," Cecile said.

"You always make such a big deal of everything," said Natalie. "Stop being such a baby and tell me how old."

"That's for me to know and you to find out." Cecile turned and started up the ramp. "They're ugly," she said in too loud a voice when she reached the top. "And they've got big ears."

"Would you be quiet!" Natalie clamped a hand over the top of her suit as she sat up quickly. She yanked the sunglasses resting on top of her head over her eyes and glared. "They'll hear you, you idiot!"

"I hope they do," Cecile said. "They deserve it."

"Cecile!" Natalie called.

Cecile kept walking. She didn't know who made her angrier: Natalie or the Interlopers. How could Natalie be interested in a boy she hadn't even seen? Cecile fairly flew up the dock.

The glare when she reached the top of the stairs halted her in her tracks. Shading her eyes with her hand, she blinked dazedly at the parking area sitting empty and calm in the midday sun.

Hope flared up in her heart. They must have heard her. Heard her being rude and climbed right back into their ugly Interloper car with their big ears blazing with embarrassment. That would teach them to go to places where they weren't welcome. Wait till Natalie heard. Who cared if she was furious?

A noise on the drive made her look. The dark car had stopped halfway down the drive. If it kept going straight, it would mean they were leaving. If it turned left, it would take them to the cottage.

Keep going, keep going, keep going . . . Cecile held her breath as the car started to roll. Then it

turned at the discreet metal sign that said THE COT-
TAGE and disappeared behind the hedge.

Their name was Cahoon. Sheba reported what she'd
learned about them from Mr. Peabody at dinner that
night as the children sat at the table in her spotless
kitchen with the black-and-white tiled floor. There
was a relaxed feeling in the air, the way there always
was when their parents went out for the evening and
they ate in the kitchen. Sheba didn't mind if they
came to the table barefoot, something that was
never allowed when they ate in the dining room.
She'd let Jack come to the table wearing only his
shorts tonight, too, and bring his little men. He'd
set them up in a circle around his plate: tiny gray
men, some crouched, others standing, rifles aimed
to protect his dinner.

Lucy rested her head on her arm between bites
and stared straight ahead. Her eyes were at half-
mast, her mouth moved slowly. No one told her to
sit up. Sheba had put their plates in front of them
in an easy, careless way, as if dealing out cards. Now

she was wiping the stainless-steel counters with slow, deliberate movements while they ate. Her gray uniform with its white collar and apron was spotless. Only the beads of sweat on her upper lip and forehead told of how long she'd stood over the hot stove.

A large fan in one corner moved lazily back and forth, sending a stream of gentle air over the group at the table and rippling the pages on the pad next to the telephone. A small photograph of a little brown-skinned boy with a wide grin sat on the shelf above it. He was Sheba's son, Joey, waiting for her at their apartment with his father until Sheba got her Sunday off.

"William's the oldest, then Jenny, then Leo," Sheba said as she put the last of the pots upside down in the drying rack.

"How old is William?" Natalie asked.

"Sixteen. Same as Harry." Sheba wrung out her dishcloth and draped it over the faucet to dry.

"How come he's not working and Harry is?" Cecile said. "He must be spoiled."

"Jenny's a year younger than you, Cecile."

"What do I care? I'm not going to have anything to do with them," Cecile said. "They're Interlopers."

"They're more interesting than anything else around here," said Natalie. She aimed her ardent gaze at Sheba again. "Cecile said they were wearing uniforms. That means they go to private school."

"So, what's so great about that?" Cecile moved her food around on her plate with her fork without eating. "They're funny looking, Natalie. You should have seen their ears."

"Private school in New York City? Do you have any idea what that means?" Natalie said, dismissing Cecile with a look of utter scorn. "What does Mr. Cahoon do?" she asked.

Sheba laughed her low, good-natured laugh. "Why?" she asked, her broad face amused. "Did this boy William ask you to marry him already? Is that why you're so interested?"

"See? Sheba knows it's snobby," Cecile said. "If William went to East, you wouldn't look at him twice."

"But he doesn't, does he?" said Natalie.

She was already planning her strategy. Cecile could see the gears of Natalie's brain turning, figuring out what clothes she would wear tomorrow, how to do her hair, whether or not she should put new polish on her nails.

As if Cecile had read her mind, Natalie splayed one hand in front of her, brought it closer to her face to examine her nails, and frowned. "I'm not hungry," she said abruptly. "May I be excused?"

"Leave your dishes next to the sink," Sheba said, flicking her eyes over Natalie's half-full plate. "I don't know why I bother cooking for a fourteen-year-old girl."

"Fourteen and a half," Natalie said happily. She put down her plate and glass and threw her arms around Sheba's waist. "Oh, Sheba, I love you," she said, smiling her dazzling Natalie smile.

"What you love is getting your own way." Sheba gently pried Natalie's hands from around her waist and gave her bottom an indulgent pat. "Go on and let the others finish."

Another flash of her radiant smile, and Natalie was gone. The door swung closed on her heels. "I'm not hungry either," Cecile said. She pushed away her plate and sagged against the back of the chair.

"Now, don't *you* start getting crazy on me," said Sheba. "This family only needs one wild girl at a time."

"I'll never be wild," Cecile said.

"You'll be a teenager yourself, same as your sister."

"I'll *never* be like Natalie."

"Nobody's saying you will. Come on, baby, I'm taking you up," Sheba said, lifting Lucy out of her chair. Lucy's head promptly flopped against Sheba's shoulder, her thumb went into her mouth. "Put your dishes on top of Natalie's," Sheba said. "I'll take care of them when I come down. You can come back for dessert when I'm done putting your sister to bed."

"Do I have to finish the rest of my chicken?" Jack called.

"It'll fly away if you don't." Sheba's voice floated back and was gone.

"You don't have to if Natalie doesn't," Cecile declared. "Come on." She put her foot on the pedal of the garbage can to hold it open for Jack and then scraped the rest of her dinner in, too. Even though I love Sheba's stew, she thought. Even though I'm still hungry. She let the lid mournfully down. Jack sat back at the table to continue his battle.

The setting sun flooded the living room. Clusters of chintz-covered couches and deep armchairs were arranged in inviting circles. The jigsaw puzzle the children worked on with Granddad on rainy days lay half-finished on a card table in one corner. Cecile's feet sank into the soft carpet as she crossed the room and collapsed onto a couch.

Picking up a magazine from the coffee table, she flipped aimlessly through it, then threw it back down. She stretched out along the couch to discover the pillow for her head was flat. Peevishly, she sat up and plumped it up and lay back down, but it did no good. Natalie's excitement had invaded her body like a germ.

The Interlopers were already ruining everything.

Natalie hadn't even seen William and she had a crush on him. No, not a crush. She had set her sights on him. That's what their father called it. He made it sound like hunting.

Tomorrow Natalie would laugh at stupid things William said that weren't funny and toss her head to make her hair fly back over her shoulders; William wouldn't be able to take his eyes off her. Cecile had seen it happen with the boys Harry brought home from prep school. Had sat in the living room, watching Natalie pretend to read, then suddenly jump up with a startled cry when the boys entered the room, as if she hadn't heard them crashing around in the front hall and been lying there, waiting for them.

A door closed quietly upstairs. Cecile pictured Lucy in her bed in their dusky room. Cecile had been happy to do that, too, when she was little. She'd lie between cool sheets and fall effortlessly into sleep to the sounds of life on the terrace. They made her feel safe.

Oh, don't be a baby, Cecile thought. Really, it was

too annoying; the tip of a feather pricking the back of her leg through the fabric of the cushion was unbearable. She got fussily up and went into the dim front hall. Standing in front of the mirror over the sideboard, she stared.

What did people see when they looked at her, with her sharp chin, her untamable hair, her eyes too wide apart? And her nose. Cecile despaired over her nose. Natalie said it was a boy's nose—straight and plain like their father's. Natalie's nose, on the other hand, was a ski-jump nose, Natalie said; she ran her finger along it lovingly to show its graceful curve. All the prettiest models had ski-jump noses, Natalie said. Cecile, glued to Natalie's side, believed every word.

Her mouth was all right, though, wasn't it? Couldn't anyone smile a dazzling smile if they practiced? Cecile smiled at herself and then frowned; smiled again to show her teeth this time and shook her head, laughing silently as if a boy had said something funny. The boy on the boat, maybe.

But no, he wouldn't fall for a phony smile.

Something about the way he'd stood there told Cecile he'd think she was an idiot if she were to smile at him that way. She could never respect a boy who would actually fall for it.

Did all boys fall for a girl's fake smile as long as she was pretty? And what if the girl wasn't pretty? What then? Surely it was only the dim light of the foyer that made her look so pale and insignificant.

Defiantly Cecile gathered her hair on top of her head and turned her face from side to side, checking to see which was her better profile. Natalie said girls needed to determine which one was theirs, and then make sure they sat on the right side when they were on a date so that it was the one the boy would look at.

Both her profiles were ordinary. She let her hair fall.

At the sound of footsteps on the stairs, Cecile looked up. "I'm going to the dock," she said as Sheba came slowly down.

"No dessert tonight?"

"No." Cecile sagged against the banister. What if she went to the dock and the boy was there, with the

Rammer and the tiny lights lining the bow sparkling in the night and the people on board laughing and talking? What would she do or say? "Well, maybe," she said listlessly.

"That's a girl." Sheba swept the stray rose petals that had fallen on the table into one hand. She wiped its gleaming surface. "You come sit with me in the kitchen," she said. "You've had enough for one day. It's time for you to be settling down for the night."

"But I'm not even tired," Cecile protested feebly as she followed Sheba's wide back through the swinging doors. The warm air rushed out to greet her.

Chapter Six

They had to come down sooner or later. Cecile climbed on a piling and held her arms out for balance. It was tricky, keeping one eye on the stairs while trying to stand as still as a statue. It wasn't the same, either, playing statues by herself. The whole point was to see who could stay frozen in their pose the longest without falling into the water.

"Yeah, right," Natalie had said earlier this morning when Cecile asked if she wanted to play. Natalie tilted her chin and held up her right arm as if she were holding a torch, the pose they used to imitate the Statue of Liberty. "Hi, William," she said in a mocking voice. "You can call me Liberty."

"We're not going to let them change everything," Cecile said.

"Maybe you're not."

Who did Natalie think she was fooling, pretending to sunbathe? The sky was overcast; the sun's weak rays held no warmth. Cecile shivered, wishing that Harry was here. Harry would play with her. He never passed up the chance to show off the pose of *The Thinker* he'd perfected over the years. Watching him stand calmly on a piling, with one leg crooked and the other leg resting on his knee, his forehead on his fist, pretending to be deep in thought, always made the rest of them laugh so hard they lost their balance long before Harry did. He won every time.

How cold the inky water looked! Cecile rubbed her thin arms. She needed to be hot before she could jump; she dreaded the shock of it even on a hot day. The rest of them always leaped ahead wildly, shouting, "Slowpoke!" and "Chicken!" to goad her on. The icy drops they splashed on her feet alone were enough to make her climb down.

People couldn't help being cautious; they were born that way. Of course, it would be worth it when she finally jumped and made it back to the surface.

But first would come the slight feeling of panic when the water closed over her head. She'd squeeze her eyes shut against the riotous, noisy bubbles and kick as hard as she could to rise up . . . up, only feeling safe again when the sun was on her face and she could breathe.

But there was no sun this morning to reward her, no jeering siblings. Cecile was about to climb down when she heard voices. Whipping her head around, she saw the Cahoon children filing down the stairs behind their mother and quickly put her foot down to steady herself. How embarrassing it would be to fall in front of them!

"Leo, come back here," Mrs. Cahoon called when Leo started toward the float with a fishing pole in one hand. He must have spotted Jack. Cecile could tell the pole and hook were plastic. Wait until Jack saw it.

Mrs. Cahoon put her large straw bag down in front of the cabanas and took out a tube of lotion. She could have been in the city, the way she was dressed. Her flowered dress was belted at the waist; a sweater hung over her shoulders. She wore a hat, too, and, oh my gosh . . . (Cecile wobbled and almost fell again at the sight of them) high heels! No one wore high heels to walk down to the dock. They'd make walking on the drive impossible. Had Mrs. Cahoon expected the Island to have sidewalks?

How funny! If only this were last summer and she and Natalie had been hiding in the lilac tree when Mrs. Cahoon wobbled by. It would have been all they could do not to laugh out loud. Mrs. Cahoon didn't look like a person who would appreciate wobbling. Maybe that was why she looked so severe and hadn't called hello to Cecile when she saw her. Because she did see me, Cecile thought, but she ignored me. And I ignored her.

Mrs. Cahoon squirted a thin stream of lotion into the palm of her hand and motioned for Jenny to turn around. What a baby, letting her mother do that. Cecile watched as Mrs. Cahoon slid her hand under the straps of Jenny's suit and ran it over Jenny's back and shoulders briskly and efficiently. When she tapped Jenny on the shoulder, Jenny turned back around and lifted her face so her mother could spread more lotion over her cheeks, nose, and forehead.

Mrs. Cahoon motioned to William next. Cecile couldn't stand it for another minute. They weren't just babies; they hadn't even been born yet.

"Geronimo!" she cried, exhilarated, and jumped.

Shocking, how dark and cold it was. Cecile burst back up to the surface, gasping. Then the thrill of it: of not being a pale, pudgy child who was afraid of the sun, and the triumph of having jumped, took over. She treaded water and tilted her head back until it reached her hairline, then quickly lifted her head up again, plastering her hair away from her face so it rested sleek and heavy on her neck.

Natalie and she used to call it their seal look. Whoever had the smoothest hair won. Now Cecile tilted her head back again and again with her back to the dock; she wondered if anyone was looking. She moved her arms and legs to make herself spin in circles. She closed her eyes. She was a mermaid.

"Isn't it freezing?"

Jenny was sitting on the edge of the dock. A

white smear ran along one side of her nose, her stomach in her bathing suit rose round and comfortable as a pillow. She was even paler and softer than she'd looked in clothes. Her brown eyes were filled with admiration.

"Not really," Cecile said. Then, "Well, sort of. It's still early." She swam quickly to the ladder and grasped a rung to pull herself up. The warm air folded around her skin as she rose.

"It's freezing," Jenny cried, putting up her hands to shield her soft self when Cecile stepped onto the dock, sprinkling water. "I can't believe you jumped from the top of that thing."

"What, the piling?" Cecile said carelessly. She adjusted the legs of her suit, shook her arms. "It's nothing." She felt Jenny's eyes on her back as she climbed up on the piling again. William passed her on his way to the end of the dock, glanced at her, and looked away.

"Is your brother girl crazy?" Cecile asked.

"You'd better believe it."

"Then he's going to like my sister."

"They'll be flirting before you know it," said Jenny.

Cecile glanced at her, alert.

"Don't you know what flirting is?" said Jenny.

"Of course I do," Cecile said, and jumped. The bubbles roared around her head as she sank down. Who did Jenny think she was, assuming Natalie would have anything to do with a boy who had such ears? When her feet touched bottom, she pushed back up.

"My sister doesn't flirt with just anyone, you know," she said as she neared the ladder.

"My brother does." Jenny watched as Cecile climbed the ladder. "Which one are you?"

"Cecile." Cecile pulled herself up, adjusting the legs of her bathing suit. "And you're Jenny and your brothers are William and Lèo." She strolled toward the piling, climbed up, shook her hair.

"How do you know?"

"It's our island."

Cecile jumped again, higher this time, and spun in the air like a top. That ought to show her, she thought smugly as she sank down, down, down.

Interloper who thinks she knows everything.

But Jenny was waiting on the edge, patient as a dog. "Can you touch bottom?" she asked when Cecile resurfaced.

"If I want to."

"Is it over your head now?"

"Of course."

"I don't like swimming over my head," Jenny said.

"Jack swims over his head, and he's only eight." Cecile pulled herself up the ladder and sat down. The dock was warm on the backs of her legs.

"I'm a total chicken," Jenny said. "I'm afraid of dogs, too. Even small ones. William calls me Chicken Little."

Chicken Little! If Natalie were here, she'd look at Jenny's stomach and make a face behind Jenny's back. Somehow Cecile didn't think Jenny would care. She felt oddly envious of the way Jenny sat there, so unself-conscious, so contented. Cecile never used to care either.

Suddenly she was glad Jenny hadn't been insulted; she was happy. "I think flirting's dopey, don't you?" she said, rolling over onto her stomach to let the dock warm her whole body.

"The girls at my school practice on one another," Jenny said, doing the same. "We don't have boys."

"What do you mean, practice?"

"You know, they dance, and one of the girls pretends she's the boy and leads. Or they practice kissing the backs of their hands and watch what it looks like in the mirror." Jenny shrugged. "Stuff like that."

"Kissing the backs of their hands?" Cecile said. "What does that do?"

"Don't ask me."

"Weird."

They rested companionably, side by side, and, cupping their chins in their hands, stared at the action on the float. Leo was watching Jack cast, with his own fishing rod dangling uselessly at his side. Jack was patiently explaining something. He held out his rod for Leo to take, keeping a careful eye on Leo when he did, and made casting motions with his arms for Leo to imitate.

William stood at the far corner of the float staring

out at the wall of sea grass, as if he found it far more interesting than Natalie lying tan and sleek behind him.

"Leo's not going to catch a fish with that hook," Cecile said.

"He wouldn't know what to do with it if he did," said Jenny. "Does your brother catch things?"

"Tons of fish. We eat them for breakfast, sometimes."

"*Eeuuw*, I hate fish," Jenny said.

"What about lobster?"

"I've never had it."

"You've never had lobster?" Cecile rolled over and sat up. This was wonderful! Jenny was afraid of deep water and had never eaten lobster. Why, she didn't know anything!

"Have you ever held a hermit crab?" Cecile asked. Then, "You *do* know what a hermit crab is."

"Those little things with shells and lots of legs?" Jenny said, sitting up.

"That could be a lot of things," Cecile said. "Don't you go to the beach where you live?"

"We mostly swim in the pool at our club."

"Pools," Cecile said. She had nothing else to say about pools.

"My mother's worried we'll step on something at a beach," Jenny said apologetically.

"Don't tell me she doesn't let you go barefoot."

Jenny hunched her shoulders in the face of Cecile's cold stare. "My father stepped on a rusty can at a beach when he was little and had to get a tetanus shot," she said meekly.

This was getting better and better.

"Your mother's not going to follow you around the whole time you're here, is she," Cecile said, "making sure you have lotion on and are wearing your sandals?"

The question felt momentous. The two girls sat, eyes locked, as it quivered in the air between them. Much depended on Jenny's answer: the direction of their friendship, or (more delicious and dramatic) if a friendship would even be made.

"She hates the sun," Jenny said. "We only came here so my father can be in a golf tournament. Mom will sit in the house all day and read. Anyway," she finished, and it was as good as a drop of blood exchanged between them, "I wouldn't let her."

There. It was sealed.

"All right, then." Cecile got to her feet. "We'll start with hermit crabs."

Jenny stood up, too. "Do they bite?"

"Not hard. I suppose you've never touched a jelly-fish, either?"

"Yuck," said Jenny, shivering, excited.

They heard a laugh and looked toward the float. Natalie was sitting up now, her hands on the straps of her bathing suit as she looked up at William, who finally seemed to have noticed her.

"See? They're already starting." Jenny's voice was breathy. "First they pretend they don't notice each other. Then they start."

This wouldn't do. Jenny hadn't sounded nearly as interested in hermit crabs.

"Who cares?" Cecile said, starting off. "Let's go. How long are you going to be here?"

"Ten days," Jenny cried, running to catch up with her.

"Only ten days? That's hardly any time. I'm sure

Lucy has some hermit crabs in her bucket."

"You promise they won't hurt?"

"They'll tickle, Chicken Little," Cecile cried as she broke into a run. "Hurry up, slowpoke!"

The girls staggered back in the late afternoon, sunburned and victorious, to show the day's bounty to Jack and Leo. The four of them crouched around the two buckets on the float, inspecting. Cecile kept her eyes on Leo as he held out his hand for Jack to put a huge hermit crab on it.

"We had to walk up and down the club beach about ten times for it," Cecile warned. "Be careful."

Leo's face was a mixture of terror and excitement, as if he were dreading the moment when the crab drew blood but was prepared to face it like a man. He would have faced anything for Jack by this point in the day. Jack was the mighty fisherman. Jack was kind.

"Don't jerk your hand away, even if it tickles," Jack said in his serious way.

"But what if it hurts worse than a needle?" quavered Leo.

"You'd better do it on the beach," Cecile told Jack. "You know he's going to drop it."

Cecile fixed the whole of her attention on the bucket. She'd spotted Natalie and William when they came around the corner of the beach from the direction of the club and quickly checked to see if they were holding hands. She let out a soft puff of air when she saw they weren't.

"Here they come!" Jenny said excitedly when their footsteps sounded on the dock.

"So?" Cecile said. "Make sure you don't hurt those minnows! Pay attention!"

But Jenny didn't want to pay attention. "I wonder what they've been doing," she said, and squeezed Cecile's arm. She'd been squeezing Cecile's arm all day, whenever she got excited. Cecile had enjoyed it earlier; it made her feel brave. Now she jerked her arm away and kept her head down as Natalie and William approached.

The weight of them standing there when they stopped at the top of the ramp bore down on the top of her head. Only when Jack led Leo up the ramp did Cecile finally look up, and then it was all right, because it was the boys she was interested in, not them.

Natalie had rolled up the sleeves of one of Harry's old shirts and tied the tails in a knot over her bikini. Her blue eyes stood out in her tanned face; her sunglasses held back her hair. The tops of William's shoulders and the rims of his ears were red. His madras bathing suit hung to his knees. The outline of his sunglasses, visible in his shirt pocket, was faintly etched against the sunburn on his face.

"They're hermit crabs," Natalie told him as he peered into the bucket when the boys hurried past. "What else did you get, Cecile?" she asked.

"A few jellyfish and a ton of snails."

"Oh, snails," said Natalie. "Whoopie."

"We got three horseshoe crabs, but we let them go."

"Where have *you* two been all day?" Jenny asked in a coy voice, looking at her brother. Cecile longed to pinch her.

"That's for us to know and you to find out," said William.

He sounded as if he were eight. Natalie knew it, but she laughed anyway, saying, "I showed William around the island."

"I bet *you* didn't catch anything," said Jenny. "Other than each other, that is," she added under her breath.

"I can get all the fish I need right here," William said. He grabbed the rope tied around a piling and started to pull it up, hand over hand.

"That's King's bait trap," Cecile said.

"I told him that this morning, Cecile," said Natalie.

The top of the bucket appeared above the water and made a great sucking noise as William pulled it clear.

"Did you tell him King doesn't like people to fool around with it?" said Cecile as William pulled the bucket all the way up to sit on the dock. "Not even people he knows?"

"Don't be such a brat," said Natalie.

"He doesn't, Natalie. You know he doesn't."

"Down, Fido! Sit!" William commanded, grinning broadly when Natalie laughed.

"King really is a beast about people touching it," she said as she rested her hand on his arm.

"I certainly wouldn't want to offend a king, now would I?" said William. He let go of the rope and pushed the bucket toward the edge with his foot. It hurtled down and slapped against the water before sinking out of sight. "Whew," William said, wiping imaginary sweat from his brow. "Maybe now the king won't behead me."

Look at them, Cecile thought disgustedly when Natalie laughed. Natalie, trying to sound like Mom, and William puffing out his chest like a silly rooster. She longed to hit him, to somehow puncture William's air of confidence and send him hurtling down, too. "You're not supposed to drop it like that," she said, her eyes blazing.

"Who's she, the dock keeper?" William said to Natalie with a rude jerk of his thumb.

"My little sister's very strict," Natalie said. "Aren't you, Cecile?"

"I'm not your little sister."

"Very strict, indeed." Natalie shook her finger in

William's face in a perfect imitation of a teacher. "If she knew half the things you said to me today . . ." William tried to grab her finger, but Natalie quickly hid it behind her back.

"I am not strict, Natalie," Cecile said loudly.

But Cecile wasn't there for Natalie, only William. When he reached around her with both arms, she twisted and turned inside his embrace as if delighting in the feel of it. Her shirt rose up as she did, and William put his huge hands on her waist. Squealing, Natalie ducked and ran laughing up the dock. William was fast on her heels.

She could have been leaving Cecile once and for all, Cecile felt so bereft. Have fun with your playthings, children, I'm gone. How *could* she make fun of her own sister like that in front of a stranger? Cecile thought as she looked blindly into the bucket. An Interloper. Everything blurred.

"I told you he was girl crazy," Jenny said proudly beside her.

It was horrible, horrible, that this pudgy girl should be allowed to think her pudgy brother was so wonderful. But for Natalie to think so, too?

"Don't do that," Cecile snapped when Jenny idly stuck her hand into the bucket, causing the minnows to dart frantically. "Now look what you did." As if no one ever stuck their hand in a bucket with minnows before! a voice in her head chided. As if they wouldn't settle down the minute Jenny withdrew her hand.

"Sorry." Jenny's voice was gratifyingly meek, but Cecile couldn't forgive her.

"You probably frightened them to death," she said. She snatched up the bucket. "We'd better get them into the water before they die. If they do, their blood will be on your hands."

What blood? Imagine! Cecile could have laughed. But Jenny had fallen willingly into the mood; her face was a tragic mask of turned-down lines. She could have been mourning the loss of a beloved hamster, with her hands so piously clasped. "I can make music," Jenny offered.

"What kind of music?"

Jenny rested her hands on the rise of her soft

belly and intoned, "Dum, dum, de-dum, dum, de-dum, de-dum, de-dum . . ."

"All right, but not too fast."

Holding the bucket out in front of her as if it were an offering, Cecile solemnly led the way to the beach. Both girls wore grave expressions suitable to conducting a funeral. Cecile knelt down at the water's edge and beckoned for Jenny to do the same. Somberly, oh, so somberly, she tilted the bucket in the shallow water until three still bodies bobbed lifelessly out.

The mourners looked at them in silence. Then, miraculously, "Made you look! Made you look!" If fish could shout joyfully, these fish would have; they sprang into life, darted away from the shore, and were gone.

"You did it!" Jenny cried, clapping. "You saved them!"

Cecile forgave her completely.

Chapter Seven

Lucy went first, clutching the bag of bread crumbs Sheba had entrusted to her care as they made their way slowly across the lawn toward the inlet. Jack walked behind her, brandishing his stick. Cecile trailed last, with Granddad. He held her elbow gently; she kept her arm bent in a stiff crook. Ice cubes clattered from the terrace as her father dumped them into the bucket at the bar. Her mother was upstairs getting dressed.

Granddad's white linen pants and shirt gleamed in the setting sun. His silver hair was slicked back from his forehead in neat, straight rows like the furrows in a field. He looked at Cecile and squeezed her arm. "Happy?" he asked.

"Yes."

Granddad's cheeks were gently bellowing in and out. Cecile had learned, over time, that it meant he was thinking. He ran a large newspaper in the city and was often preoccupied. He had a black phone in his study that he got important phone calls on; no one other than him was allowed to answer it. When the children were young, they often stood in the doorway and stared at it, as if expecting it to explode.

Granddad's driver, Jimmy, came and went throughout the month, delivering messages and important papers. On Sunday, he'd drive Granddad and their father back into the city, where they'd spend the week at their jobs before Jimmy drove them back to the Island on Thursday night. Cecile felt proud to have Granddad to herself now; proud but anxious. She wondered whether he would talk to her and ask her questions. She dreaded disappointing him. She was happy to skirt the corners of adult conversation and know him in that way.

"Red sky at night, sailor's delight!" Jack called back as they neared the water.

"Take Lucy's hand," Cecile said officiously.

"She won't let me!" he reported.

"Lucy . . . ?"

At the sound of Granddad's voice, Lucy took Jack's hand. There were rules to be followed, even when it came to feeding the greedy clutch of seagulls Granddad called his "pals."

"What do you say we go feed my pals?" he'd say when he came down from taking a shower after golf. "Anyone interested?" He'd look around uncertainly, as if they didn't all rush to join him every summer, night after night.

"How can they be hungry when they steal food from people's picnics and smash those poor defenseless mussels against the rocks all day?" their mother would protest. She said seagulls were worse than rodents, but Granddad loved them.

His pals had seen them coming. As if summoned by a dinner gong, dozens of them had materialized in the inlet and hovered over Lucy and Jack, screeching and laughing as they darted and swooped.

"Can we start?" Jack asked when they came up to him.

"Go ahead," said Granddad.

Jack's first piece flew straight up and was attacked by several gulls. Lucy threw her entire handful, all at once. The pieces scattered on the ground in front of her like confetti.

"Not like that, Lucy," said Jack. "One at a time. Like this."

He bent his knees and then shot straight up, leaning back as he hurled the bread high over his head. A seagull picked it neatly from the air before it could start back down. Cecile took a few pieces and threw them out over the water. Granddad threw his one at a time, carefully, like Jack. He handed his last piece to Lucy and said gravely, "Let's see what you've learned, Lucy."

Lucy tossed it. It rose hopefully into the air and dropped back down, bouncing off her hair onto the ground, where a gull hopped over and nabbed it.

"Better watch out for those curls," Granddad told her solemnly. "My pals might think they're worms."

Lucy clamped her hands over her head and ran in

delighted circles, shrieking. "Seagulls don't eat worms," Jack tried to tell her, but Lucy was giddy with the idea of her hair, alive. She started back up the lawn toward the house, zigzagging crazily, with Jack running behind her, waving his stick, a loyal sheepdog directing a stray sheep back to its pen.

Their mother stood up from where'd she'd been watching and walked toward them over the grass. Lucy grabbed her mother's hand and shook her head vigorously; her hair flew out around her like sparks. Her excited voice, raised in explanation, floated through the evening air.

"What've you been telling Lucy, Dad?" their mother said laughingly as Lucy and Jack raced up to the terrace. "More of your nonsense?" She linked her arms through his and pulled him against her, smiling back quickly at Cecile as if to say, Mine, all mine. She leaned her head against her father's shoulder; Granddad planted a kiss on the top of her hair.

It was almost dark. Ahead of them, the house was coming alive. Candles flickered in small lamps scattered on the tables around the terrace. Cecile could see Sheba through the French windows. She was moving slowly around the living room, stooping to turn on lamps, to straighten a magazine, to fluff a pillow. She picked up an empty tray from the sideboard and moved back across the windows to stand in the screen door, a dark silhouette.

"The children's dinner is ready," she announced through the dusk.

"Thanks, Sheba." Their mother let go of Granddad's arm and led Lucy over to the door as Sheba swung it open. "Would you make sure Lucy washes her hands, please. There's no telling what germs those horrible pals of Mr. Hinton's carry around." She turned and beckoned to Jack and Cecile. "Come on, you two. Sheba worked hard to cook you a wonderful dinner."

"I'll go up and get Natalie," Cecile said.

"She went down to the dock." Her mother ushered Jack through the door and kept it held open. "She forgot something, so I told her she could go and get it. You go ahead and eat. Natalie can have hers later."

"What'd she forget?" Cecile said.

"I don't know. Come on now. Don't keep Sheba waiting."

"I'll go get her."

"Cecile!"

But Cecile was walking away on stiff, determined legs around the corner of the house. "I'll be right back!" she cried, breaking into a run. She sped across the grass.

Natalie didn't forget anything. She was meeting William, Cecile was sure of it. Just because she was fourteen, she was acting like she was old enough to skip dinner with the babies and meet her *boyfriend*. How dare her mother act as if Cecile should eat early but Natalie didn't have to?

Cecile flew down the drive in the deepening dusk, an avenging angel. And there they were: standing together at the end of the dock with their shoulders almost touching as they watched the sun setting over the bay.

"Natalie!" Cecile shouted as she ran toward them. Natalie quickly shoved something into

William's hand as she turned around. William bent and put it on the dock behind a piling.

"What are you doing here?" Natalie said, her face tight with defiance.

"What's that?" Cecile asked, craning to look. Whatever it was, it had made Natalie nervous. Cecile's own nerves tingled with her sister's alarm. Then, "You're drinking beer?" Cecile said, incredulous.

William stepped quickly in front of it.

"It's not mine," said Natalie. "It's William's."

"But William's not allowed to drink either."

"God, your sister's a pain," William muttered. He turned and raised his foot, bringing it down angrily on the can to flatten it. "Beer? What beer?" he said as he kicked it over the side.

"You can't do that!" Cecile cried. "Natalie, tell him."

"You're the one who made him do it," Natalie said, her face flushed. "If you'd minded your own business, he wouldn't have."

It seemed impossible. That Natalie would still side with him against her. "It's time for dinner," Cecile insisted. "Mom said to come get you."

"Tell her I'll be up in ten minutes."

"She said to come now."

They stood glaring at each other, eyes locked, the way they had when they were little. But she wasn't going to be the one who backed down anymore; she was too old. "What else were you doing?" Cecile said accusingly.

"Nothing," Natalie said, tossing her head.

"Nothing?" said William. "Thanks a lot, Natalie." He grabbed her arm and started dragging her toward the edge of the dock. "I'll show you nothing," he said.

"Don't you dare!" Natalie shrieked, planting her feet and straining against him. "I'll get my hair wet!"

"Nothing, huh?" William repeated heavily.

"Kick him in the shins!" Cecile shouted.

William had to be a lot stronger than Harry to be dragging Natalie the way he was. Natalie was an expert on not getting thrown into the water. She and Cecile both were. Harry had tried a million times. Now William was inching Natalie closer and closer to the edge. His face looked positively scary: His cheeks and neck were flushed. His mouth hung open to reveal huge teeth.

Cecile grabbed Natalie around the waist and pulled.

"Let go!" Natalie's face when she rounded on Cecile was so full of fury, Cecile dropped her hands. Natalie surged forward again, shrieking louder than before.

"Take it back," William ordered her, his open mouth glistening. "Say you were having a fascinating conversation."

"I was having a fascinating conversation!" Natalie shouted. She showed all of her teeth, too.

"The most fascinating in your whole life?"

"The most fascinating in my whole life!"

"All right then." When William stopped pulling, Natalie sagged gratefully against him. She shut her eyes and put the palms of her hands against his chest, as if exhausted.

But she wasn't exhausted at all; she'd loved every minute of it. Natalie had pretended to be weak so

William would feel strong. Even more amazing to Cecile was the fact that William actually believed it. He looked so smug, so proud.

Natalie, leaning against him, watched Cecile through narrowed eyes and looked every bit as victorious.

It was all a game.

"You're not coming up, are you?" Cecile said.

"Tell Mom ten minutes," said Natalie.

"Tell her yourself."

Her legs might have turned to stone, they felt so heavy. Cecile walked away from them without looking back. She heard William laugh and knew he was laughing at her. They were both laughing at her. She walked stiffly up the steps.

The sun had set. The sky was black. Cecile located the three stars of Orion's belt and the Little Dipper above her head. A screen door slammed at the pump house. A phone rang. Fireflies flickered the length of the drive.

Why was it that sounds made at night seemed so much sharper, so much more full of significance, than those heard during the day? It was all soft, reassuring sounds when the sun was out: the faint cries of seagulls, the hum of distant lawn mowers, the heavy buzzing of bees feeding on the privet flowers.

Natalie, drinking beer. Better not to think about it. Whatever she did, she couldn't tell her parents. There'd be a scene; scenes couldn't happen on Gull Island. Maybe she should say she'd seen William drinking beer; that might work. Their mother would warn Natalie to be careful. Cecile felt suddenly desperate that someone warn Natalie to be careful. Quickening her pace, she shouted out with relief, "I found her!" as she rounded the corner of the house. Then, abruptly, she halted. The intensity of the floodlight in the corner was startling, yes, but it wasn't that. Something was odd here, too.

The terrace looked empty. All of the hustle and bustle of preparing for dinner was gone. No. Someone was lying in the far, dark corner on Granddad's lounge. Cecile stood, blinking dumbly, as the reclining figure broke apart and became two.

"Where's Dad?" Cecile said in confusion when she saw who it was.

"Is something wrong?" King's arm slid from around her mother's shoulders as she stood up. "Is Natalie with you?" her mother said.

"She's at the dock." Cecile couldn't stop her eyes from darting between her mother and King; they had a life of their own. "Where's Dad?" she cried.

"For heaven's sake, Cecile. You made it sound as if something terrible had happened." Now that her mother wasn't worried, she was impatient. "Your father's inside. What difference does it make?"

"But what were you doing?" Cecile said. "What's King doing here?"

"Excuse me?"

"It's just . . . I thought . . ." Cecile's voice trailed off in the face of her mother's scornful eyes. "It's just that Dad and Granddad were here when I left," she went on in a faltering voice.

"You're rude." Her mother's voice was ice.

Cecile looked down, her face burning.

"I'm afraid I'm imposing on your parents' goodwill

again tonight and staying for dinner." She looked back up to meet King's kind eyes gratefully as he came up behind her mother. Another set of gleaming teeth in a huge smile. But this was King. Surely she could trust King?

"Anne," he said quietly as he rested his hand on her mother's arm. "It's all right."

"No, it's not." Her mother shook off his hand. "She was rude, and she knows it."

"She's only a child," King murmured.

"I am not a child," Cecile said.

"Then stop acting like one," her mother said, smiling the satisfied smile of a cat who'd successfully trapped her mouse, "and go and have your dinner."

"That's where I was going," Cecile said. Her hands were clenched as she walked to the door. Back stiff, she opened it and went inside. Banished, like a bad little girl, to eat with the other children in the kitchen.

But Jack and Leo weren't in the kitchen, only Sheba. "People in this family are behaving badly," Cecile said as she flung herself into a chair.

Sheba laughed. "You sound like your grandfather," she said, shutting the refrigerator door.

"Well, they are." Cecile kicked the chair legs. "Natalie's at the dock, flirting. You might as well throw away her dinner."

"You just hold on to yourself," Sheba said, "and don't worry about your sister."

"Who says I am?"

"Nobody has to say a word." Sheba opened the oven door and slid out a plate. "You've been my worrier all your life."

"I have?"

"Since you were a tiny thing." Sheba lifted the lid off a pot on the stove and began spooning food onto Cecile's warm plate. "Lord, the way you used to carry on. About the snails Jack tried to take back to Connecticut in his bucket, and the fact that lobsters were still alive when I put them in the pot . . ." Sheba shook her head.

"I still think it's cruel."

"You even worried about ants," Sheba said. "I never will forget the time you rescued a whole bunch of those ants that were ruining your grandfather's rose garden with their tunnels and hid them in your bedroom."

"Granddad put down ant traps," Cecile said. "He was going to poison them."

"Red ants were running all over the house for the rest of that summer." Sheba chuckled. "Your grandfather was fit to be tied."

"I didn't get punished, though," Cecile said contentedly. She wrapped her legs around the legs of her chair as Sheba put the plate in front of her.

"That's because I never told anyone about the paper bag with a few red ants, as dead as doorknobs, I found in your pajama drawer," Sheba said.

"I know."

"You go ahead and eat now," Sheba said, resting her hand on Cecile's shoulder. "I hope you're hungry."

"I could eat a horse," Cecile declared.

"Did you rat?" Natalie asked as she stuck her head around the edge of their bedroom door.

Cecile looked up from her book. The lamp on her

bedside table was a soft spotlight in the dark room. Lucy slept soundly in shadows on the other side. "No."

"Good." Natalie ran across the room and jumped onto Cecile's bed, jiggling it merrily, as if trying to coax Cecile out of her sulk. "You'll never guess what," she said.

"What?"

"King's taking us on the *Rammer* tomorrow. I saw him and Sis downstairs."

"Really?" Cecile shut her book and sat up.

"And look what I smuggled," Natalie took a large white dinner napkin out from under her shirt and put it on the spread between them. She unfolded it ceremoniously, revealing treasure. A tiny jar of caviar and a stack of paper-thin crackers.

"Mom will kill you," said Cecile.

"No one will even notice." Natalie rocked back and forth on her bottom as she unscrewed the cap and held out the jar. "There's tons of it down there."

They spread the tiny eggs with their fingers,

determined to ignore the sharp saltiness of a luxury their parents coveted so highly. Shouts of laughter and the clinking of ice cubes floated up from the terrace.

"Who else is down there?" Cecile asked.

"The Whites and some couple from the club I don't know."

Someone put on a jazz record. Cecile turned off her light and they knelt in front of the open window, pressing their noses against the warm screen, to watch.

"Sis looks tipsy again," Cecile said after a few minutes.

Tipsy is what their mother had said Sis was a few summers ago when Sis had started shouting on their terrace one night and their father had had to walk her home.

The children had watched as Sis leaned against their father's shoulder and yelled, "The king is dead, long live the king, the pitiful SOB!" and then laughed.

"S, O, B spells sob," Natalie had said excitedly.

"Oh, *sob, sob!*" The children had rubbed their fists in their eyes, pretending to cry, as they rolled on the floor. When they asked their mother about it the next morning, she said Sis had eaten something that didn't agree with her and it had made her tipsy. The children had laughed again to hear such a silly word.

"It means drunk, you know," Natalie said now.

Cecile stared.

"You didn't know that, did you?"

"I did too."

"You know what else?"

Cecile shook her head.

"That isn't lemonade in Sis's thermos. It's liquor."

Cecile was shocked. "How do you know that?"

"William."

"What does William know?"

"We saw Sis one afternoon when she was leaving the beach. William could tell she was drunk."

"It's none of William's business," Cecile said. Then, in spite of herself, "Did you get drunk on that beer?"

"Don't be an idiot," Natalie said, jabbing her.

"Don't you be an idiot," Cecile said, jabbing back. "What does drunk feel like, anyway?"

"Sob, sob!" Natalie joked, rubbing her eyes.

Her sister's laughing face was so close, her friendly glance so familiar, Cecile didn't ask how Natalie could bear him. She looked out at the party; she didn't even want William in the room.

Chapter Eight

"Model walk," Natalie commanded.

Cecile took one of the towels she and Natalie were carrying down to the dock and carefully balanced it on her head. Keeping her back stiff and her eyes straight ahead, she walked as steadily as she could, the way models walked on runways in fashion shows. She and Natalie used to practice at home using books. On the Island, they used towels and had contests to see who could make it down to the dock without losing theirs.

With their colorful towels piled high, their arms laden with canvas bags and more towels, they could have been the leaders of a caravan crossing the desert. Lucy and Jack had run on ahead with their father. Their mother and Granddad were bringing up the rear.

The drive was warm beneath Cecile's feet; the hamper banged rhythmically against her legs. "Mom said we're having lunch at the Hungry Pelican again," she said over her shoulder. She pictured the white stucco restaurant perched on the hillside above the bay and the tall foamy drinks with umbrellas King had ordered for them last year. "King said he bought bigger inner tubes. I can hardly wait to ride them."

When her towel threatened to slip to one side, Cecile tilted her head. To be going out on King's boat at last! She'd stand in the bow as they roared into the bay and pretend to be the masthead, holding her face into the wind as they cut across the water. Waves would part helplessly under the bow while small boats zigzagged ahead of them. When the sun got too hot, she'd sit under the awning and watch her father, Granddad, and Jack fish.

She was so busy picturing the day that when she reached the top of the stairs and saw the boy standing with his back to her at the entrance to the boat-house, she halted. He jabbed a metal scoop into the ice cooler, again and again, and let the cubes clatter into one of the two buckets at his feet. The other bucket was full.

One last scoop and the second bucket was full, too. The boy tossed the scoop into the cooler and let the lid slam shut. Cecile saw the muscles in his arms flex as he bent down and picked up a bucket in each hand. She could count the ribs in his tanned, shirtless back. Her heart was pounding in her ears, as if something had leaped out at her in the dark and terrified her.

"Don't stop here," Natalie said impatiently as she came up behind. "Nobody can see where they're going."

"Sorry."

The boy glanced their way as he turned. His eyes slid over Cecile as if she weren't there and rested, for a fraction of a second, on Natalie, before he walked away. She might have been a ghost, the way he'd looked through her, Cecile thought, but he'd seen Natalie. And when they got on the boat, Natalie would see him. A surge of jealousy so strong she thought she might get sick surged through her. And of her own sister.

"Get *going*," Natalie said, prodding her in the back.

Ahead of them, the boy jumped nimbly onto the deck of the *Rammer* and went below. How could she go on the boat now? Her, in her tank suit, next to Natalie in her bikini. Oh, and her chest! Cecile's towel tumbled from her head when she looked down. Maybe she could run back and get a shirt.

But if she left, she wouldn't be there when Natalie and the boy looked at each other. Wouldn't be there to stop Natalie from smiling and tossing her hair. To stop the boy from smiling back. The boy wouldn't have eyes for anyone else.

The day suddenly felt excruciating.

"Cecile! Natalie! Look!" Jack waved proudly from his perch on a blue inner tube in the stern like a prince on his throne. Lucy sat next to him on an orange one, a beaming princess. "King said we can write our names on them!" Jack shouted.

The boy came up from the cabin and went to the far side of the boat. He moved slowly toward the prow, leaning over to check that everything was in order. Natalie jumped nimbly onto the deck and dumped her towels on the low table under the awning. She fell onto the couch and rested her foot on her knee, hunching over it to inspect it.

"You made me stub my toe, you idiot," she said. She touched the bloody flap of skin dangling from the tip and winced. Pushing up her sunglasses, she leaned back and rested her foot on the edge of the table. "Why'd you have to stop like that?" she complained, shutting her eyes.

The boy had rounded the bow and was moving toward them. Cecile glanced up when he went past; he kept his eyes straight ahead as he stepped onto the dock. He nodded to Granddad and her mother as the three met halfway down the dock and kept walking. Cecile's legs went limp.

"Watch out!" Natalie cried as Cecile sagged onto the cushion beside her. She pulled her knee to her chin again to inspect the damage. "Haven't you done enough harm?"

"I think that was the new cabin boy," Cecile said.

"Who?"

"The boy who was just here."

Natalie looked up, saw no one. "So? Do you have a crush on him or something?"

"I'm not *you*, Natalie."

"You do, don't you?" Natalie said. She took a last look at her toe and lowered her foot to the deck. "I wouldn't get too excited. He's not coming with us."

"How do you know?"

"King told me last night that he was going to have us all to himself." Natalie made a mocking face. "Poor Cecile."

Poor Cecile, indeed. It was all she could do not to cheer when the truck's engine sprang into life in the parking area and the pickup rolled slowly out of sight.

"You and your cabin boy can row your dinghy up the East River and come visit me and my husband on Sutton Place," Natalie was saying as she twisted her hair into a knot on top of her head and fastened it with a clip. "Although you'll probably have to use the service entrance."

Of course! She should have realized—the boy

could notice Natalie all he wanted. Natalie wouldn't pay any attention to a boy who worked on a boat.

Oh, joy, oh, bliss! "First dibs on the blue tube after Jack!" Cecile shouted as she leaped up and ran to greet Granddad and her mother. "Mom," she called. "I hope you brought the root beer!"

They got back to the dock at three, full of salt air. Natalie went up to the house with their mother and Granddad. Cecile stayed behind with Jack to watch King and their father clean their fish on the fish shelf attached to the side of the boathouse. Cecile always watched, as much as she mourned for the poor fish. First they scraped off the iridescent scales with a flat of a knife. Then King used his long, thin knife to effortlessly slice off the head of each fish underneath the gills. Last came the guts. They scooped those out callously, with a single finger, and dropped them into a bucket.

Cecile and Jack carried the bucket to the rocks and emptied it for the gulls, then Cecile went up to the house. Natalie was standing outside their parents' closed bedroom door. She put a finger up to her mouth and beckoned to Cecile to join her.

"A letter came from Harry while we were gone," she whispered when Cecile stood beside her.

"And I say he can stay there until his contract's up," they heard their father say.

"Contract? What contract?" their mother said. "He's sixteen, in case you've forgotten, Andrew."

"His commitment then. It's not going to kill him, being unhappy." Cecile pictured her father's cold, remote face. "If anything, it might teach him a bit of discipline."

"You and your damned discipline." There was silence, and then the sound of the bathroom door closing with a controlled slam. Natalie and Cecile hurried down the hall to their room.

"More drama, thanks to Harry," Natalie said when she'd shut the door. "If I were you, I'd stay as far away from them as possible."

For once, Cecile didn't argue.

Chapter Nine

"We're not going anywhere until you take off those shoes," Cecile said when Jenny finally came down to the dock at nine thirty the next morning. (Nine thirty! What could she have been doing?)

"My mother made me," said Jenny.

"All the more reason." Cecile stood over her like a sentry until Jenny revealed her soft, white feet.

"Now what?" Jenny said as she followed Cecile tentatively down the steps.

Cecile took pity on Jenny and led the way in the shallow water at the sand's edge. "Is that the boat you went out on?" said Jenny.

"Yep."

"Is it your grandfather's?"

"No, it's King's." Cecile had given the *Rammer* enough of a glance to see the boy was unloading supplies from the wagon he'd pulled down the dock and carrying them down into the cabin. "Stop staring," she told Jenny, picking up her pace. "It's rude."

"But did you see that boy?" Jenny asked in an excited whisper as she trotted to keep up. "Ooh la la. Who do you think he is, the prince?"

"Don't be such an idiot."

"He's cute. Do you know him?"

"Why should I?" Cecile said. "Come *on.*"

It was going to be a scorcher. Already the heat was sharp on their shoulders; the tiny waves lapped at their feet like soothing cats' tongues. Cecile led Jenny to the pile of rocks at a far end of the beach. The craggy outcrop was exposed, twice a day, by the falling tide, its uneven surface a combination of slippery seaweed and rough barnacles.

The pools of clear water left behind in crevices and cracks were like small lakes, and the girls like giants; they stepped over miles of countryside in a single stride; they peered into the depths of each one and saw clear to the bottom. Anything might be found in a lake—a rock that sluggishly tilted and moved, revealing itself to be a snail. Crabs, of course, and mussels, clinging to the sides, impossible to tear free. Once in a while, if they were lucky, a starfish.

Cecile could have been a savage child raised in the forest by wolves, compared to Jenny; Jenny was as soft as her feet. She was afraid there were ticks in the sea grass or that she might step on the sunken tail of a horseshoe crab as they wandered along the shore. She even hesitated to hold the piece of pale green glass Cecile showed her that had been sanded to a smooth surface by the waves and sand.

"It's harmless sea glass," Cecile said impatiently. "We have a whole bottle of it at home."

"It's still glass, isn't it?"

When they left the beach and roamed the island, it got even funnier. Cecile had to pull Jenny back by her blouse when she started to topple over after Cecile showed her how to balance on the railing of the bridge; she shrieked and flapped her hands in front of her face when a lazy bumblebee hovered in front of them as they walked past the privet hedge.

"Stop yelling," Cecile said, shooing it away. "He couldn't sting you if he tried. He's ready to burst!"

By the middle of the day, even Cecile had to admit the driveway was hot. They walked on grass where it was available, and ran quickly where it was not as they made their way back to the dock. The way Jenny hopped and shrieked, lifting up her feet like a man in India walking across hot coals, made them laugh so hard they collapsed onto the grass and rolled around for minutes and minutes, delighting in the feeling of it. All it took was for Cecile to imitate Jenny's shrill "Ouch! Ouch! Ouch!" to set them going again.

They didn't hear the car coming. Sis slowed to a stop as the girls lay, panting, and rolled down her window. "Are you all right?" she asked in a disapproving voice. Cecile was about to sit up when Sis added, "You're not disabled, I hope?"

It set the girls off again; they couldn't help it.

"Silly girls," Sis said, and drove slowly on.

"Who was that?" Jenny asked.

Of course, then Cecile had to tell her the story about King and Sis. Jenny listened with such an avid, hungry look on her face, Cecile almost immediately regretted having opened her mouth. "I can hardly wait to see what King looks like," Jenny said in a breathless voice when Cecile was finished.

"He looks perfectly normal," Cecile said. What had she been thinking, telling Jenny? If Jenny told her mother, Mrs. Cahoon might look down on King and Sis. How dare she? Cecile thought, feeling her hackles rise. She doesn't even know them.

"You have to promise you won't tell anyone," she told Jenny fiercely. "Not your mother, or your father, or anyone."

"I won't. I promise," Jenny said. Then, delighted: "My mother would have a fit."

"You mean like this?" Cecile fell over onto her back and lifted her feet in the air. "Ah . . . ah . . . ah!" she cried, flailing her hands and feet about wildly, picturing Mrs. Cahoon doing the same thing, but in high heels. Jenny laughed, even though it was her mother Cecile was making fun of.

"Come on," said Cecile finally. "I want to show you something."

Darn, the pickup truck was still in the parking area. Cecile had become conscious of her every move when the *Rammer* was docked. Thankfully, the boat, dock, and beach were all empty; the still air was hazy with heat. Anyone with a lick of sense was inside eating cool melon or drinking iced tea. It was all blissfully deserted.

But for how long, if the truck was there? The boy and Captain Stone might have gone out fishing or into town to buy supplies. What if she and Jenny were standing here when the boy came back?

"Come on," Cecile cried as she ran down the steps and crouched beside the dock. "Hurry up!" she said, beckoning to Jenny as she ducked her head and crawled under. "Before someone sees you."

"Like who?" Jenny protested. "There's no one here." But she ducked down and crawled under the dock, too.

Cecile scooted up on the hard-packed sand toward the concrete footing that secured the dock until her head almost touched the dock's wooden slats. The air was thick with the sharp smell of mud and salt. The low tide was heading back in.

Cecile loved hiding here. When they were all little, it was where they ran the minute they heard a boat. Here Harry, Natalie, Cecile, and Jack would huddle as the feet of strangers pounded over their heads. Last summer, Harry had deserted the game to play golf and Natalie had become too fastidious. Even Jack, who in his own way was as particular as Natalie, never came here anymore.

As for Lucy, she'd been convinced a monster lived there ever since the day Cecile had made growling noises as Lucy walked overhead.

"What're we going to do under here?" Jenny protested as she struggled to crawl on all fours while using one hand to keep her nostrils pinched firmly shut.

"Hide," Cecile said when Jenny finally plopped onto the sand beside her.

"But it's disgusting," Jenny said. She frowned at the bits of shells and wet sand clinging to the palms of her hand before wiping them off on her shorts. "Why does it smell so bad?"

"The tide's out. Shhh . . . don't talk so loud."

"There's no one around. Who're we hiding from, anyway?"

"Just wait," Cecile said. What did Jenny *do* in the city, anyway? She didn't understand the first thing about mystery and excitement. "If you'd be quiet for one minute," Cecile said with a touch of contempt, "you'll see something amazing."

"One minute," said Jenny, but she didn't sound happy. Cecile could almost see her counting the seconds in her head.

It was amazing, really, how quickly the tide came in. If you were willing to sit patiently and watch, you could see it eagerly lapping against the pilings, the waves edged with a hem of seaweed and foam. Cecile sat quietly, hoping that Jenny would too. But Jenny shifted restlessly, rocking from side to side to get comfortable, until Cecile was finally forced to order, "Sit still!"

"I can't help it. This sand's as hard as a rock," Jenny said. "How much longer?"

Before Cecile could answer, the amazing thing she'd been waiting for happened: A tiny hermit crab poked up its head from a hole in the sand in front of them and poised on the edge with its feelers darting tentatively, ready to dash back into hiding at a moment's notice. Sensing the coast was clear, it slowly began waving a claw back and forth in the air as if calling surrender with a white flag.

Immediately a second crab crawled out, and then a third. A fourth, fifth, sixth.

The wet sand between Jenny and Cecile and the water was soon cluttered with them. Cecile put her finger up to her lips when she felt Jenny look at her, not daring to take her eyes off the army that had begun moving across the sand.

But not for long.

"Ow!" Jenny suddenly cried, and each crab darted into the hole nearest it and was gone. "Something bit me," Jenny said as she fell against Cecile. "I think it was one of those horrible *things*." She brushed frantically at her bottom.

"It's probably a shell," Cecile said. She shrugged

Jenny off in disgust. "Look what you've done. They're gone. You ruined it."

"I don't care." Jenny got up onto all fours. "I'm getting out of here."

"Not yet!" Cecile cried. She grabbed Jenny's leg. "Listen!"

It was a boat. Cecile and Jenny froze as the sound of it approaching the dock grew louder and louder. A boy's voice called out. Another boy's voice answered. Jenny looked at Cecile questioningly as she settled back on the sand. Cecile shook her head.

The boat slowed as it neared the dock. Whoever was driving cut the engine. Cecile heard the boat knock against the wooden pilings as it slid into its spot. There was a thud of feet as someone jumped up onto the dock.

"Wind it around that one," a voice called. "Right. Now make a slipknot."

Oh, no. Her heart pounding, Cecile ducked to look beyond the pilings. The boy grabbed the small motor of the dinghy with both hands and yanked it up so that the propeller blades lifted clear of the water. When Jenny tapped her on the shoulder, Cecile sat back. Who? Jenny mouthed, raising her shoulders. Cecile dumbly shook her head.

The oars clattered together as the boy stowed them under the seat of the boat. "That should do it!" he called. Then he leaped onto the dock, too, and the two boys started toward shore. Their voices and laughter rose and fell, their footsteps stumbling from side to side as if they were knocking against each other.

The boys in Cecile's school walked the same way: pushing and shoving and knocking into one another in the halls like mountain goats jockeying for space on a narrow mountain path. One time when they slammed Cecile into her open locker as they passed, she indignantly told them that, that they looked like goats.

"Yeah, horny as goats," one of them had said, and the other boys laughed. She could tell it meant something dirty.

"Oh. My. God," Jenny mouthed as they came closer, her eyes popping with excitement.

The space between the boards over Cecile's head suddenly felt as wide as a window. If the boy were to look down now, he'd see her—crouched on the sand like a little girl, hiding. She didn't dare to look up.

"What about the blonde?" she heard the other boy, not her boy, say. "She's pretty hot."

"If you like that type."

"What's her name?"

They were almost overhead now.

"I make it a point never to ask." Cecile pictured the boy's careless shrug. "It drives them nuts. Those rich girls all have the same kind of name. Anyway, they're too much work for me."

The other boy said something about cars as they walked on. There was a series of thuds of things being tossed into the boathouse—life preservers, probably. Then their feet on the steps, and the door of the truck slammed. Then the other door, and the engine started up. In the thunderous silence that followed the sound of the truck leaving, Cecile heard her heart pounding in her ears. She felt even Jenny could hear it.

They were talking about Natalie, they had to have been.

"Who were they?" Jenny asked breathlessly.

"I don't know," Cecile said. "Day trippers, probably."

"Maybe it was that boy from the boat."

"So?" The space was suddenly too small. Jenny with her eager, hungry face so close to Cecile's. It was horribly cold, too. A chill ran through Cecile's body from her head to her toes; she was desperate for the sun. "Let's get out of here," she said, and scrambled off. Only when she was standing on the beach, with the heat of the sun on her shoulders, could she breathe.

"That would have been so embarrassing if they saw us," Jenny panted, standing up next to her.

"Why?"

"Oh, my god. Two boys?"

"They'd think we were clamming," Cecile said coldly. "That's what people do on beaches, in case you don't know."

"But two boys?" Jenny insisted. "And you and me, crawling out on our hands and knees?"

"Boys, boys, boys," Cecile said. "I'm sick of it." She looked around to find something, anything, to deflect Jenny's attention. Looking down the beach, she had never been so happy to see her little sister.

"Cecile! Cecile!" Lucy cried. Her high-pitched voice floated across the beach like a lifeline as she raced toward them from the direction of the club. Sheba walked slowly behind her, carrying a large canvas bag and a beach chair. Jack trailed behind Sheba. He was dragging their striped umbrella and stopping more than he walked to pick up interesting shells and strings of seaweed the water had deposited at his feet.

"Cecile! Cecile!" Lucy cried again. Her voice was joyful; she ran as fast as she could to see her very own big sister on the beach.

"Lucy! Lucy!" Cecile raced to meet her and swooped Lucy up, swinging her in dizzying circles that made Lucy shriek. When Cecile finally put her down, Lucy staggered drunkenly down to the edge of the water and sat with her legs straight out and her knees pressed tightly together. She raised her shovel above her head, prepared to beat back any wave that dared try to drag her out to sea.

Cecile threw herself on the sand as Sheba approached. "They didn't want to stay at the club," Sheba said, putting the bag next to Cecile and slowly unfolding the chair.

"Who can blame them?" Cecile said, squinting up at her. "There's much more to do here."

"And I guess you found it." Sheba gave a deep sigh of contentment as she sat down and stretched out her legs in front of her, kicking off her shoes. "Judging from the look on your face," she added.

"My face?" Cecile said. What did Sheba see? How could she possibly know? And what a horrible time for Jenny to arrive! Cecile furiously wiggled her eyebrows at Jenny as if sending a message in code. Say nothing! her eyebrows ordered. "We haven't been doing anything, *have* we, Jenny?" she said.

"Us?" the willing accomplice replied innocently. "We've been sitting around."

It was a perfect lie because it wasn't really a lie— it just wasn't the whole truth. Sneaky Jenny. But oh, my. The way Sheba was looking at her. It was as if she could see right through Cecile's skin.

"Come on!" Cecile shouted as she jumped up.

"Where're you going now?" Sheba asked.

"Nowhere!" Cecile cried, dragging Jenny across the sand in her frenzy to get away.

"Mmm, mmm, mmm." Sheba shook her head, watching them go. Then, "You going to get over here any time today with that umbrella, Jack?" she called.

Jimmy drove Granddad and their father into the city after golf. They wouldn't be back until Thursday night. The children and Mrs. Thompson stood on the front steps while Jimmy loaded suitcases into the trunk, waving good-bye until the car disappeared down the drive. Then they turned, in one motion, and went back into the house. Opening the screen door, they discovered it had become a household of women.

Even the walls seemed to have let go of their upright posture to breathe more easily—the air in all the rooms was relaxed and quiet. For four days, there would be no male voices calling for coffee or announcing their arrival. The smell of cigarettes would be gone from the terrace. There was a relaxed, carefree feeling in the air that the presence of one small boy would do nothing to disturb.

"Poor old Jack," Mrs. Thompson said laughingly.

But Jack burst out from the kitchen shouting, "Hot dogs and hamburgers for dinner! And Sheba made ice cream!" and they all filed after him onto the terrace to eat with their fingers, lounging on chaise lounges, bare feet and all, their mother too. If fireworks had suddenly exploded in the sky over the inlet as they sat there with night falling, it wouldn't have struck any of them as odd; it felt like a celebration.

Cecile had thought they'd all watch television with their mother, but after they'd taken their dishes into the kitchen, and Natalie said, "I'm going to the dock for a while," Cecile announced she was too. She looked at her mother, reading to Lucy and Jack, when she reached the door and asked, "Will you be here when we get back?"

"If I'm not, I'll only be at the Pump House."

"Oh."

"Does that meet with your approval?" her mother asked coolly, looking up from the book held open in her lap.

"Sure. I mean . . . sure," Cecile said, and hurried to catch up with Natalie in the front hall.

"What are you going to do, spy on me again?" Natalie said.

"I can go to the dock whenever I want, Natalie."

"Well, don't follow me," Natalie said, pushing through the screen door. She let it go behind her. Cecile caught it before it slammed.

"There's only one way to get to the dock, you know," she yelled, but she took her time, letting Natalie get farther ahead. By the time Cecile arrived, Natalie and William were sitting on the rocks. Music played on a radio on the *Rammer*; the boy was swabbing the deck.

Cecile lay on the dock with her head hanging over the edge so that anyone watching her would think she'd spotted something fascinating in the water.

Like what? she thought, feeling more and more like an idiot as the night got darker and she went on lying there. Where would she go if she stood up? She could hardly see the water now, much less anything fascinating in it. She must look as if she was dead.

Then feet pounded on the dock and Jenny cried, "What are you doing?" so Cecile rose quickly to her feet. Good old Jenny, she thought, meeting her halfway.

"My parents had people in for drinks, so I snuck out," Jenny said proudly.

"Did you stuff pillows under your blanket to make it look like you?" Cecile asked.

"I probably should have."

The night felt suddenly exotic. The sun had sunk; the air was cool. Cecile was deathly aware of the boat and the boy; they pulled at her like a magnet. She didn't know in which direction to walk.

"Let's go to the float so we have to walk past the boat and that boy will notice us," Jenny said.

"No way!"

"Who's Chicken Little now?" Jenny said, flicking her hair. "Come on."

A quick, bold feeling surged up in Cecile. Terrified to follow, she couldn't stay behind. "Don't say a word," she whispered furiously when she caught up. She gripped Jenny's arm above the elbow. "I'm warning you. . . ."

Jenny laughed and pulled her arm away. "Why, Cecile Thompson!" she cried in an exaggerated voice, hoping to be heard as she skipped on ahead. "If you aren't the funniest thing!"

Two could play at this. "What about you, Jenny Cahoon?" Cecile cried, running up behind. She grabbed Jenny's hand, they pushed and pulled, giggled and shrieked.

"I know," Jenny said when they stopped to catch their breaths. She paused dramatically. "Let's go skinny dipping."

Skinny dipping! Cecile felt the cold water on her naked body. "You're crazy!" she said, amazed.

"I will if you will," Jenny said, making as if to unbutton her blouse.

"Don't you dare!"

They darted after each other and stopped, swung their hips, prancing like tarts, or how they imagined tarts might prance. Exhilarated one second, Cecile was appalled the next. She wanted to be seen; she dreaded being noticed.

Were people looking? Let them look; they were giddy with their own daring. Cecile didn't dare even glance at the *Rammer* as they staggered past.

"Looks like someone's having a walloping good time," said a voice.

The girls shrieked and clutched each other's hands to see the man, standing on the *Rammer,* smiling indulgently at them. When she saw who it was, Cecile was instantly mortified.

"Hi, Captain Stone," she said in a meek voice. She yanked her hand out of Jenny's and slunk down the ramp to the float. Sitting on the edge, she plunged her feet into the water and knew the shock served her right. How could she have been so immature?

Jenny padded down the ramp behind her and sat down, too. "That boy didn't even look," she said, disappointed. "He went downstairs."

"Good," Cecile said, looking straight ahead. She didn't even have the heart to correct her and say "below."

Cecile introduced Jenny to the silent game the next day. According to the Thompson rules, they weren't allowed to talk to anyone: not the grown-ups or any of the other children. They couldn't let themselves be seen either. If they heard anyone coming, or saw anyone, they had to run away and hide.

Her mother had wanted Cecile to go to the club. She was playing in a tennis tournament. Lucy and Jack were taking swimming and tennis lessons. When Natalie came downstairs, looking very pleased in her yellow golf skirt and sleeveless blouse, with her hair pulled back with a ribbon to match, Cecile was more determined than ever not to go.

It felt as if they took forever, finding all of their equipment and getting organized. Cecile stood, champing at the bit, as they finally piled into the car. "You can stay today," her mother said as Lucy and Jack climbed into the backseat, "but one of these days you need to play some tennis. And Dad wants you to take golf lessons." She held up her hand to ward off Cecile's objections. "You don't have to play well, but you do need to be able to carry on an intelligent conversation about the game."

"Yes, and look interested when boys talk about it," Natalie said. She finished inspecting her face in the mirror on the back of the visor and flipped it up. "Unless you want them to think you're a total bore," she said, flashing a superior smile.

Any boy who wants to talk about golf would be a total bore, Cecile longed to say. Instead, she said to her mother, "After Jenny leaves."

"All right." Her mother shut her car door and turned the key in the ignition. "But no swimming at the dock and don't bother Sheba."

"What about lunch?" Cecile called as the car rolled slowly away.

"She'll fix you a picnic!" Her mother gave her a flutter of her hand out the window and called, "Have fun!"

Then the driveway was empty. Cecile headed for the dock.

* * *

First, she led the way along the path behind King's house. She and Jenny crouched in the tall grass and stared up at the Pump House's terrace, hoping something would happen. The only person who came out was Mrs. Harris. She shook out her mop and then snipped the dead flowers off the plant in one of the planters and threw them into the grass before she went back inside.

After, they walked to the bridge, but no one was around. "This is no good," Cecile said. "Everyone's at the club. Let's go eat lunch."

Jenny stood off to one side as Cecile pressed her face against the screen door to the kitchen. She put on a woeful, hungry look so she wouldn't have to talk, and scratched. Sheba looked up at her from the pile of silverware she was polishing at the kitchen table and smiled. "I was wondering when you two would turn up," she said. She put both hands on the table and pushed herself up. "It's been awful quiet around here."

She took two sandwiches wrapped in white paper

napkins from the refrigerator and handed them out the door to Cecile along with a thermos and two paper cups. "Think that'll hold you?" she asked.

Cecile nodded vigorously.

"You still playing that game?" Sheba said.

Extremely vigorous nodding.

"Like night and day, you and your sister, I swear." Sheba shook her head as she turned to go back to her task. "Leave the thermos on the steps," she said. "You can knock two times if you want more. Wouldn't want you to break any rules."

Her lazy laughter floated after them as Cecile and Jenny went across the lawn and into the still, hot air inside the lilac bush. Dappled sunlight filled the space the children had so carefully cleared over the years. Stumps of branches pruned long ago ringed the dirt floor. Cecile put her sandwich on one and sat on another. Unscrewing the top, she poured pink lemonade from the thermos into the two cups and unwrapped her sandwich. Ahhh . . . soft white bread with a layer of mayonnaise and crisp slices of lightly salted cucumber. They were still cold, too, and crunchy. She knew they'd be crunchy.

"Are you going to the dance at the club?" Jenny asked as she pulled the two pieces of bread apart to see what was inside and wiped off the salt with a finger.

"Salt's the most important part," Cecile said.

"I don't like it," Jenny said, biting into her salt-less sandwich. "I'm *dying* to go," she said, "but my mother said I have to be thirteen. Two more years."

"My mother's making me go," Cecile said.

"Lucky you."

"Dances aren't such a big deal." Cecile started on her second half. "I've been going to them at my dancing school for years. They're boring."

"Those aren't the same," Jenny said. "You have to wear gloves at dancing school so your sweaty hands won't leave stains on your partner's clothing. Your skin's actually going to touch a boy's skin at the club." She leaned closer, her eyes huge. "Two naked, sweaty hands, touching," she said slowly.

There it was again—that avid, greedy look on Jenny's face. "You're crazy," Cecile said. "I'm not holding anyone's sweaty hand. I'll make them wipe their hands on their pants."

"You wouldn't dare."

"Of course I would," Cecile said in a voice made superior by how much Jenny longed to go. "I have to get a new dress and everything," she said carelessly.

"You'd better buy one with back shields, that's all I can say," Jenny said.

"How about a sponge? Boys could wipe their hands on it."

They said more silly things, loose and careless. When they'd eaten every crumb and drunk every drop, Jenny jumped up. "We played the silent game all morning. It's my turn to come up with something."

Cecile wadded up the napkins inside the cups and put them on the grass outside the lilac with the thermos. When she came back, Jenny was standing on one of the low stumps. She'd taken off her hair clips; she lifted her face and shook her pale, short hair out, as if she had long tresses of gold. "We're princesses," she said in a dreamy voice, "locked in a tower, waiting for our princes to come save us. Mine is called Jean Pierre."

"Jean Pierre?" Cecile said, laughing, but Jenny was into her role: She pressed her face into the branches and gripped them tightly, as if they were iron bars. "Jean Pierre! Jean Pierre!" she cried. "Save me!"

"Save you from what?" Cecile said.

But Jenny was in a frenzy and wouldn't be stopped. Shaking her hair, she cried about her mean stepmother, her cruel imprisonment. Only Jean Pierre, her handsome prince, could save her! There was emotion in it, and passion. Jenny's sobs sounded almost real; she was nearly hysterical.

Waiting for a dumb prince, indeed! Cecile was determined to be the person in charge of the castle's stables and ran to get a horse. She galloped around on the grass in wider and wider circles; she whinnied and reared.

"Jean Pierre!" Jenny called from inside the tower. "Kiss me! Kiss me!"

The horse stopped, bored. It was embarrassing, the way Jenny's face had become bright pink and she kept rattling the branches like that. "I don't want to do this anymore," Cecile said, dropping onto the grass in the deep shadow of the elm.

Jenny came out of her tower and sat next to her, radiating heat. "The girls in my school play that all the time," she said, panting. "We do it in the girl's bathroom, where there really are bars on the windows. When people on the street look up, we duck."

"The girls in your school are weird," Cecile said.

"We don't have boys," Jenny said, shrugging. "If we did, you'd probably hear this all the time in the halls." She held the back of her hand up to her lips and made loud smacking noises.

"Are you crazy?" said Cecile. "I go to a school with boys. No one kisses in the halls."

"I bet they do but you don't see them."

"I think you've got sunstroke," Cecile said.

"That's what they were probably doing last night, you know," Jenny said.

"Who?"

"Natalie and William. You don't think they talked out there all night, do you?"

"Don't be an idiot." Cecile plucked a blade of grass and put it between her thumbs. She blew, but nothing happened. "Now, what're you doing?" she said irritably when Jenny jumped to her feet.

"Watch this."

Jenny turned around and wrapped her arms around her chest so Cecile could see her back and her fingers, gripping her shoulders. "Mwah! Mwah!" Jenny said, wiggling and writhing.

"What *are* you doing?" Cecile said.

Jenny shot a coquettish smile over her shoulder. "It's you and that boy, making out. Isn't that hilarious?" she said. "S-E-X. Haven't you heard about making out?"

"You're crazy," Cecile murmured. It was amazing and slightly embarrassing, Jenny's sudden transformation from a pudgy, eleven-year-old girl to . . . well, to something else.

"And how about this?" said Jenny.

She twirled back around and stood poised with her face very still, as if she were going over something inside her head. Then, taking a deep breath that she let out noisily through her nose, she tucked her hair fussily behind both ears as she said, "I've only done this a few times," and put her hands on her hips. She jutted one hip out to the side. "It's something else the girls at my school do."

Jenny turned her head to one side, and then whipping it back around fast so that her hair flew across her eyes, she started to chant: "Go back, go back, go back into the woods . . . 'cause you haven't, you haven't, you *haven't* got the goods . . ." With every "haven't," she made a cutting motion with her hands crossed over each other in front of her stomach as she stepped backward. "Now you may have the spirit and you may have the pep . . ." She started forward again, jerking her thumbs over her shoulder to accent the words, swinging her hips. "But you haven't got the team that the blue team's got!"

It was silly, yes, but it was also fascinating. The words sounded peppy, but the way Jenny was moving her body wasn't peppy at all. It was inviting, almost. She sounded as if she was mad at someone but was egging them to come forward at the same time.

It was a teasing game, that's what it was. You could move your body to make someone feel a certain way even if the words were different. Cecile especially liked the "go back!" part and "you haven't got the goods." There were a few people she'd love to tell that to.

"Do it again," she said as she got to her feet and put her hands on her hips. "But do it slowly this time, so I can learn the words."

Chapter Ten

"Mrs. Cahoon said Jenny can't go until she's a teenager," Cecile said.

"I fail to see how that can possibly affect us." Her mother slid the mascara wand out of the tube and leaned closer to the mirror. "Your grandfather's on the board and you're going."

Cecile sprawled on her parents' bed. She was watching her mother, who was in her bathrobe and was sitting in front of her dressing table. Steamy air from the bathroom drifted in moist and fragrant tendrils into the room. Natalie sat on a low stool beside her mother, as close as she could get. She stared raptly at her mother's face, trying to memorize every brushstroke.

"Will there be an orchestra?" Natalie asked.

"There'll be live music of some kind, I imagine. . . ." Their mother's voice trailed off as she moved the brush up over her eyelashes again and again. She sat back to look; she leaned forward and applied more.

"Fabulous," Natalie breathed. Whether she was enchanted by the orchestra or her mother's hypnotic motions, Cecile couldn't tell. Probably both, knowing Natalie.

Even Cecile watched in silence. She knew, from having watched her so many times, that her mother had to keep her mouth open ever so slightly while she did this part, and not talk. Whether it was to stop from poking herself in the eye, or so that she could concentrate, it looked like a delicate maneuver. Both girls kept a respectful silence.

The moment her mother sat back, Cecile said, "The boys' hands will be all sweaty."

"What has gotten into you?" her mother asked, fluttering her eyes at herself in the mirror. "You act as if you've never been to a dance before. It'll be fun."

"It'll be more than fun. It'll be fantastic. Why do

you think we've been taking dance lessons all these years?" Natalie jumped up and started waltzing around the room with her arms held out as if for a partner. "One, two, three . . . one, two, three . . . oh, you're so marvelous!" she drawled, throwing back her head to smile up into the face of an imaginary boy. "You're the funniest boy I've ever met!"

"No one says marvelous except in movies," Cecile grumbled. "Boys will think you're crazy."

But Natalie was above her, floating on an air of romance with a boy so real, Cecile could almost see him. He would have his hand planted possessively in the middle of Natalie's back. His eyes would be staring down into hers. Natalie could say anything she wanted. No boy would willingly let her go.

"Marvelous, marvelous, marvelous!" Natalie chanted.

"That's it." Cecile sat up and crossed her arms over her chest, feeling as grouchy as if she were five. "If that's the way we're supposed to talk, I'm not going."

"You can talk any way you like. Talk in pig Latin,

if that's how you feel," her mother said. She twisted her tube of lipstick, making a glossy stick of bright scarlet rise up. "When I was a little older than Natalie," she said, deftly painting first one half of her lower lip and then the other before she went on, "I went to dances at West Point all the time. Sometimes two or three in the same weekend."

"Did you really?" Natalie dropped back down beside her mother, breathless and deadly serious. "Your mother let you?"

"For one thing, I was sixteen. For another, she had a fit." Their mother blotted her lips on a folded piece of Kleenex. "The day after a photograph of me wearing a strapless dress appeared in the newspaper, my mother sent me off to a girl's Catholic boarding school. I've told you that story."

"I know you have. I love it." Natalie had picked up her mother's hairbrush and was running it slowly through her own hair. "Do you think the Cahoons will be invited?" she asked casually.

"You mean *William* Cahoon," Cecile said.

Natalie shot her a withering look.

"Granddad arranged a guest membership for them while they're on the Island. I suppose they will."

The heavy brass knocker on the front door rapped loudly. King's voice called out.

"Good heavens, look at the time," Mrs. Thompson said. She got up and went over to her closet. "Natalie, run and tell King I'll be ten minutes. He can fix himself a drink while he waits."

Cecile wandered over to the dressing table and ran her hand lightly over the tubes and jars. There was the expensive lotion she'd used. She opened the lid of her mother's jewelry box and looked at the jumble of necklaces and earrings as carelessly intertwined as the lures in Jack's tackle box. Pulling the stopper from a bottle of perfume, she dabbed the stopper behind each ear and put it back. Her mother was making little noises to herself. Cecile heard the repeated thud of shoes as she picked up a pair and discarded it, wrong for whatever dress she was wearing.

"Does Dad know you're going out with King?" Cecile called.

"I'd hardly call it going out with him." Her mother came out of the closet with a yellow linen dress draped over one arm and lay it on her bed. "King and I were practically in diapers together. As you well know," she said. She slipped her robe off her shoulders and let it slide down her body; it pooled like a silk puddle around her feet. Against the whiteness of her slip, with its delicate lace bodice, her dark hair looked almost black.

"You're getting pretty dressed up," Cecile said. "Does Dad know you're going out with King *again*?"

"What on earth is wrong with you?" her mother said, turning to give her an appraising glance that wasn't altogether loving. "I don't like the way you've been acting. Are you feeling all right?"

"I'm fine," Cecile said. But she wasn't fine. All this talk about the dance, and the brushing of hair and delicious smells in misty air . . . it was as if there were an itch, deep inside her body, and all Cecile wanted was to rub up against the rough bark of a tree to scratch it; throw it off, somehow, like an itchy wool coat. But even that wouldn't take care of it; it felt a part of her.

"Am I pretty?"

The words were out before she could stop them. Cecile ducked her head. How mortifying, to hear her question in the quiet room! Imagine what Natalie would say. She willed her mother not to laugh.

"All of my children are good looking," Mrs. Thompson said, flashing Cecile an inclusive smile before she slid the yellow dress over her head. She wiggled her hips to help it fall as she turned around. "Zip me up, would you?"

Cecile stood still, as if waiting for more.

"Cecile?" her mother said impatiently, looking back. "Now, please."

Her mother slipped her arms under her heavy hair and lifted it off her neck as Cecile slid the zipper smoothly up her back. "King will have a fit if we're late to the Parkers'," she said.

Cecile felt as pale and insignificant as a moth in her mother's bright light.

*   *   *

The stores lining the main street of the village were either ivy-covered brick or stucco. Huge latticed windows jammed with clothing and jewelry, shoes and antiques, begged for attention. Wraithlike women walking small dogs on leashes lingered and stared. It all looked fake, Cecile thought as she followed her mother and Natalie down the street. Behind those facades, saleswomen were waiting to pounce the minute you walked through the door. Saleswomen who could sum you up at a glance.

Those glances were enough to freeze Cecile in her footsteps. She hated going into these shops on the days when their mother was getting her hair done or having a manicure and she let Cecile and Natalie wander on their own. Cecile would have been happy to look in the windows, but Natalie ruthlessly dragged her into every store that interested her and promptly deserted her as she breezed right past the cool voice of the saleswoman who asked, "Can I help you girls?" in a voice meant to discourage them.

A bell tinkled when her mother opened the door

of the shop. The saleswoman looked up from behind the counter and, sweeping her eyes quickly over Natalie and Cecile, rested them on their mother. "How're you ladies today?" she asked, smiling.

"Fine, thanks." Mrs. Thompson flashed a smile of her own.

"Let me know if you need any help," the saleswoman said, and went back to looking through the pile of receipts on the counter in front of her.

The shop was small and bright and reeked of perfume. The lettering over the window had announced that it was Peony Whitfield Dresses, Fifth Avenue, New York. It sold the dresses everyone was talking about this summer. At least, Natalie said everyone was talking about them.

"She's wearing a Peony," she'd said admiringly, more than once, as she flipped through a magazine at home. Their mother had told them at breakfast that that was where they were going to shop. Natalie had practically fainted.

So, what's so special about them? Cecile thought petulantly as she trailed behind Natalie and her mother. They all looked the same to her: plain shifts in bright fabric with butterflies and flowers. Pink and green or blue and yellow or blue and green. Some had white bows above the side slits; others had white trim around the neck or arms.

She was determined to hate them.

"I love these dresses," Natalie whispered as she whirled around to face their mother with a blue-and-yellow dress held up against her body. "This is so wonderful."

"What's so wonderful about them?" Cecile said. "They don't even have sleeves." She dragged her hand along the tops of the dresses, letting each one slide away from under it as if she didn't care.

"Cecile, please."

Cecile dropped her hand.

"You behave better than that," her mother said.

"I don't see why Natalie's making such a big deal about them. They're all the same flowered pattern."

"It's the fabric. The fabric's fabulous." Her mother pulled out a dress and held it up to her face, breathing it in before she held it out to Cecile. "Smell."

"Who do you think I am, Harry?" Cecile cried, stepping back. Harry always tried to make her smell his dirty sweat socks. He loved the smell of them; he said they smelled manly.

"Oh, for heaven's sake. I sometimes forget how horrible you are to shop with." Her mother clicked the hanger disgustedly against the metal rack as she hung the dress back and gave Cecile a firm, encouraging push. "Go take a look while I help Natalie. Green and blue would look lovely with your coloring."

Good. She was glad she was horrible to shop with, Cecile thought as she drifted to the far end of the row. She didn't even know she had a coloring. Just to be perverse, she pulled a pink-and-yellow dress off the rack and stood with it in front of a mirror. She held it against her body with her arm cinched at the waist to get the effect, the way Natalie did.

"Yuck," she said, and lowered it quickly. She didn't know why pink and yellow should make her skin look so much redder and her hair almost orange, but they did. She hung the dress back on the rack and chose a green-and-blue one. She held it up in front of her, too, prepared to reject it at a moment's notice.

This one didn't look nearly as bad. In fact . . . "I'll try this one," she said begrudgingly as she came up behind her mother.

"Perfect. It'll be great on you." Her mother briskly opened the door of a dressing room before Cecile could change her mind and, closing it behind her, said, "Shout if you need help."

The overhead light glared; the floor-length mirrors on three sides stared critically. There were probably people standing behind them, watching her. Cecile turned her back and tore off her T-shirt and shorts. Stepping into the dress, she pulled it up over her body. The fabric was cool and crisp against her skin. It *did* smell different; she recognized the perfumy smell she'd noticed when they'd entered the store.

For a startling second when she turned back around—as quickly as a sprite in a fairy tale might flit from one tree to another in an enchanted forest— she glimpsed a pretty girl with brown eyes under dark brows in a wide forehead and a mass of curly hair. The girl's dress was so simple, it made her long legs and arms appear more delicate and shapely than Cecile's ever could.

Cecile stared.

"How does it look?" her mother called, and the sprite was gone. Cecile opened the door and stepped into the aisle.

"I knew it would suit you," her mother said. "You look terrific. Doesn't she look terrific, Natalie?" she called, spinning Cecile around. Natalie had chosen the pink-and-yellow fabric. With her bright, sleek hair, she looked like a luscious dish of ice cream. She turned from admiring herself in the mirror long enough to cut her eyes at Cecile and say, "Too bad she can't do something about her hair."

"Oh, pooh to you, Natalie." Mrs. Thompson squeezed Cecile's shoulders and said, "Don't pay any attention to her. Your hair's your crowning glory. Go take your dress off so I can pay for it."

The mirrors seemed so much friendlier! Cecile twisted and turned. Putting her hands on her hips, she posed; she felt so free and easy inside this dress.

Maybe that was what made an expensive dress worth paying for: knowing you looked great in it made you feel relaxed. Why, she wouldn't be surprised if she sounded more fascinating at the dance.

Best of all, the thing that was making her hold her head a little higher, made her smile and show her teeth without laughing, was the fact that Natalie was jealous. Because she *was* jealous—Cecile had seen the quickest glint of the fact in Natalie's eyes when she'd turned around.

It wouldn't last for long; Natalie had plenty of crowning glories of her own. But still. Cecile stretched her arms above her head, as contented as a cat. What *was* a crowning glory, anyway?

"Your dress is so *lovely* with your coloring, my dear," Cecile drawled from the backseat on the way home. "Why, thank you, Rhett," she answered in a high voice. "You look mah-velous yourself tonight."

"The day a boy calls you 'my dear,' I want to hear about it," said Natalie.

"Frankly, Natalie, I don't give a damn."

"Cecile! Mom, did you hear her?"

"What?" Cecile was giddy with laughter. "It's from *Gone with the Wind*."

"Leave her alone." Their mother smiled indulgently in the rearview mirror at Cecile sprawled along the backseat. "You two run up and hang up your dresses when we get home, and we'll go for a swim at the club."

Cecile followed Natalie up the stairs, into their bedroom. She hung her dress next to Natalie's in their closet, only to have Natalie roughly push hers to one side to leave a wide space. "What are you going to wear under yours?" she asked as she sauntered over to their dresser and picked up her brush.

"What do you mean?"

Natalie gave her hair a few strong strokes and put her headband back into place before she turned and said, "Don't you think it's time you started wearing a bra?"

"You're not the boss of everything, Natalie," Cecile said. Her hand had gone up to her chest. Her cheeks blazed.

"I don't see why you make such a big deal about

it," Natalie said, shrugging. "Every girl has to get one sooner or later."

"I will when I want."

"I wouldn't wait too long, if I were you," Natalie said lightly as she put her brush down. "You're kind of showing, if you know what I mean."

It was artfully delivered. The cut was so quick, Cecile could only stand with her mouth open as Natalie pulled her swimsuit out of a drawer and left the room. She hardly noticed Jack when he ran past her as she walked slowly down the stairs to the front hall, either. Her mother, in her tennis dress, was kneeling by the front door fastening Lucy's sandals.

"I think I'll stay here," Cecile said to her mother's bent head.

"Are you sure?" Her mother patted Lucy on the bottom and said, "You're all set. Go get in the car," before she stood up and looked distractedly around the front hall. "If it's not in your room, you left it in the car!" she called up to Jack. "Natalie? Are you ready? I have a court at one o'clock."

"I'm sure." Cecile stepped back as Jack ran down

the stairs with his towel over his shoulder and bolted past them out the screen door. "I got them," Natalie said, holding up a fistful of magazines as she came out of the living room. "I'll be outside."

"You're slouching," her mother said. Cecile arched her back away from the quick twist her mother gave with her knuckle in the middle of Cecile's back. "That's right, stand up straight. You'll ruin the lines of your dress if you hunch like that."

"Speaking of the dress," Cecile said. "What will I wear under it?"

"Under it?" her mother said, slinging her tennis racket in its case over her shoulder and checking her face for a last time in the mirror. "Underwear, I guess," she said absently. She patted Cecile's cheek as she went past. "Don't worry about it. You'll look great."

Cecile stopped the screen door with her foot as it swung shut and sagged against it as her mother went around to the driver's side of the car. "When will you be back?" she asked.

"We should be home around five," her mother

said. "If you decide to join us, Mr. Peabody can bring you over."

"Bye," Cecile said, but it was lost in the sound of the car starting up. She watched until it was gone and then went into the kitchen. Sheba was sitting on the back steps, husking corn. The drying yard, ringed with tall hedges to conceal the clothesline, was to the left. Tall white lattice walls hid the garbage cans on the right. It was always strange to see Sheba out of uniform. In dark blue shorts and a sleeveless white shirt, her large arms and legs looked as warm and comforting as pillows. She wore old loafers, several sizes too big, on her bare feet. The bag was half full of husks and silk; Cecile saw Joey's photograph on the step beside her.

"Whose shoes are those?" she asked, her face pressed against the screen.

"I thought I heard someone." Sheba lay an ear of clean corn on the pile of other ears on the dish towel in her lap. "They're Oscar's," she said. Oscar was Sheba's husband. "Make me feel like home."

Cecile stood watching as Sheba deftly stripped

the husks away from the corn and picked off the strings of silk, one string at a time. "Want some help?" she asked after a while.

"I'd never say no." Sheba shifted over and moved Joey's photo to her other side so Cecile could open the screen door. Cecile saw Joey's smiling face and huge dark eyes and thought about how he'd be leaping around on the train platform beside Oscar, barely able to keep still, when Sheba's train pulled into the station on Sunday.

Sheba told them all about Joey when they ate in the kitchen: how he was always waiting for her, every single time. How he always had a new painting for her to admire and sometimes a new space between his teeth.

"And kisses?" Sheba would say, laughing. "That boy has the biggest kisses in the whole world for his mama."

Cecile felt a pang in her heart as she sat down, to think about Sheba having a little boy who she looked forward to seeing so much. A cute little boy, who would hug Sheba fiercely around the neck with his skinny arms when he saw her and refuse to let go. She probably wouldn't think about the Thompsons until she was back on Gull Island.

Now that she thought about it, Cecile realized mournfully, she'd never kissed Sheba and Sheba had never kissed her. Not even once. She sagged against Sheba's broad shoulder, letting her ear of corn dangle listlessly between her knees.

"What's on your mind, girl?" Sheba said, giving her a quick glance.

"Nothing."

"A heavy kind of nothing." Sheba finished that ear and put it down and picked up another one.

"Mom brought Natalie and me new dresses for the dance tomorrow night," Cecile said.

"So I heard."

Cecile watched Sheba strip one leaf . . . two. . . . "I don't have anything to wear with it," she said.

"Your mother told me you were getting new shoes."

"I don't mean shoes. I mean anything to wear *under* it."

"Oh. *Under* it." Sheba finished with her last ear

and took Cecile's half-shucked ear out of her hands. "What'd your mother say?" she asked, starting on that one.

"She was late for her court time."

"I'm sure she would have done something if she'd had the time," Sheba said. She put the last ear of corn on top of the pile and tied up the ends of the towel. "I have to go into town with Mr. Peabody to pick up a few things for your mother anyway," she said as she put her hands on her knees and pushed herself up off the step with a groan. "You go on upstairs and put on some shoes. You and I can do a bit of shopping of our own."

"And buy what?" Cecile asked, her heart beating very fast.

"And buy you a bra," said Sheba. "Isn't that what we're not talking about?"

The saleswoman in the lingerie department looked up. Sheba was moving majestically toward her with her leisurely stride, in her pale gray uniform, like an ocean liner coming into dock; Cecile followed gratefully in her wake. The saleswoman stood up behind the counter as they approached. Her eyes flitted expectantly between Sheba and Cecile, as if uncertain where to land.

"What can I do for you ladies today?" she asked.

Sheba gestured for Cecile to stand beside her. "This here is Cecile Thompson," she said with her arm resting lightly around Cecile's shoulders. "She's a granddaughter of Mr. Hinton at Gull Island."

"Mr. Hinton. Of course." The saleswoman directed the full force of her beam at Cecile. "How can I help you, Cecile?"

"Cecile's going to a dance tomorrow night at her grandfather's club," Sheba said. "She needs a bra and panties to wear under her new Peony."

Cecile looked up, astonished. Sheba stared straight ahead.

"A new Peony! My, what a lucky girl," the saleswoman said.

"Two sets," Sheba went on. "Something feminine, with a bit of lace, and another set in white for under her day clothing."

Day clothing? Her new Peony? The saleswoman was hanging on Sheba's every instruction; Cecile didn't have to say a word. It all could have been happening to someone else, she felt so unembarrassed.

"Of course," the saleswoman said smoothly. It was her turn to put her arm gently around Cecile's shoulders, as if Cecile were some delicate creature who needed to be protected. "Come with me, Cecile," the saleswoman murmured. "We'll find you exactly what you need."

Sheba gave the slightest nod of her head when Cecile looked back. Like a queen, Cecile thought dazedly, as she let the saleswoman lead her away. Sheba. A queen.

"Thank you, Sheba," Cecile said. She clutched the shopping bag tightly to her chest as she slid onto the backseat of Mr. Peabody's car. It was over. They had done it. And now, Cecile owned one set of beautiful pale blue underwear with lace, and a pretty white set. Panties, she thought with an inward blush. She was full to bursting; she could say no more.

"You're welcome," Sheba said from the front seat. "People surely are impressed by a name, aren't they now?" she added, shaking her head. "Mmm . . . mmm . . . mmm."

Chapter Eleven

Some of the boys she'd danced with had had hot, sweaty hands, but not this one. Even so, Cecile wanted to yank her hand away from his and hide it behind her back. He was barely holding on to it, but letting it lie loosely in the palm of his hand, which was insultingly dry. His other hand felt like a clamp on Cecile's back: huge and unmoving. His closed, aloof face said he wasn't the least bit interested in talking.

Cecile could have been a mannequin, for all he seemed to care. Ever since meeting her eyes for a second when the chaperone had bossily pushed them together, he'd been looking over her shoulder as if searching for something more interesting to watch. He'd stayed like that for the entire dance, without even once having to look at his feet.

Cecile had put her hand on his shoulder, the way she was supposed to, and followed his feet, counting in her head. One, two, side-together, side, back-step. They were playing "Mack the Knife," a foxtrot.

So much for the advice Natalie had given to her about talking to boys when they were getting ready earlier in the evening. "Any boy can be made interesting if you ask him questions," Natalie had instructed with her face close to the mirror and her mouth hanging open, ever so slightly, an exact replica of their mother's as she applied her mascara. "But don't look too interested. Boys don't like girls who run after them."

"How can I ask questions without looking interested?"

"You'll get good at it. Just remember that there's no such thing as a boring date. It's up to the girl to make it exciting."

"I'm not going on a date," Cecile protested. "Probably no one will even ask me to dance."

"They have to. One of the chaperones will make them."

Cecile had dressed in the bathroom, frowning as she tried to fasten the clasp of her bra. Her arms ached with the effort, she felt foolish and clumsy. Why should girls have to wear something that feels like a belt around their chests? she thought, twisting. Still, what she saw in the mirror made her hold her head up, put her shoulders back.

She'd put on the simple sandals her mother had bought, combed her hair and tucked it behind her ears with the hopes that it would stay there, brushed her teeth, and was finished. Natalie had spent an hour in the bathroom and another half hour in front of their mirror.

"Now, Mom's mascara," she said, and Cecile dashed willingly down the hall to snatch it off the dressing table and run back. Natalie didn't even need it, her eyelashes were so long and black. Her full mouth didn't need the pink lipstick Natalie put on, either, and her cheeks were already glowing with excitement.

She really was very pretty, Cecile had to admit. She sneaked a quick look at her own face in the mirror and thought that Natalie's excitement must be catching—her eyes and face looked so much more vibrant than usual. Even her hair seemed to be cooperating.

"I still don't see why it's the girl's responsibility," Cecile said.

"It just is." Natalie's eyes met Cecile's in the mirror. "Anyway, you look good in that dress. Maybe no one will recognize you for the slob you really are."

"I am not a slob," Cecile said, laughing.

It had been impossible to be mad at each other. The new dresses and shoes, the important way their mother had let them eat in their bedroom, in their bathrobes, after they'd taken their baths. Sheba had brought up their dinner on a large tray and put it on the low table under the window. "Big night," she said, smiling, as she turned to go.

Lucy had begged to be allowed to stay and watch, but their mother had lured her away with the promise of a trip to pick up Granddad at the club and an ice cream from the snack bar at the pool.

"What kinds of questions?" Cecile asked.

"Oh, anything—what his name is, what school he goes to, what sports he plays."

"What if he doesn't play sports?"

"They all do. They wouldn't admit it if they didn't." Natalie finished with the mascara and handed it to Cecile. "Run get Mom's rouge. I'll put a little on your cheeks to make your cheekbones stick out."

A lot of good it did, having her cheekbones stick out. This lunkhead wasn't even looking at her; Cecile wasn't about to talk to his chin. He didn't have to act as if dancing with her was such a misery, either, stiffly leading her around the way he was, without bothering to look at her. He was probably conceited because he had such beautiful eyes. Why should she ask *him* questions? Why didn't he ask her something?

It was starting to feel as if he was dancing with her under orders, his back was so stiff, his arms held at odd angles as if cemented into place. Was she really so horrible that all he wanted was to get through this dance so he could race over to his friends lined up along one wall and join in whatever it was that was making them laugh?

"I don't care what your name is," she told him. "I'm not going to ask, so don't expect me to."

She glared over his shoulder at the boy and girl dancing behind them. At least Cecile had a partner who was taller than she was; the girl behind them towered over hers—a hunched, miserable-looking boy with slicked-back hair and a blazer with sleeves that hung over his knuckles. He disappeared inside it; from the look on his face, he wouldn't have minded disappearing altogether.

Cecile's partner showed no signs of having heard but soldiered gallantly on. His big, fat hand was probably leaving a mark in the middle of her new dress, too. How long would this dance go on? She should have said no when the beaming chaperone with her beaming fake face had pushed her and this stranger together, crying, "Have a lovely time, children!" Who were these women, anyway, who circled the floor, prepared to turn any dancer unlucky enough to try to escape back into the ring?

"I don't care what your name is, either."

The boy's face was blank. Maybe she hadn't heard what she thought she'd heard. Cecile mustered through a few more steps before saying, "And I'm not going to ask you what sports you play. You'd probably just lie."

He snorted. At least, it sounded like a snort. Cecile looked up at his face again and felt a smile playing around her mouth. She forced it into a disapproving thin line and stared over his shoulder. She could look as disinterested as he could.

Order was breaking down around the room. One couple had given up trying to keep time and was marching determinedly around the room with the boy pushing the girl backward in a most ungentlemanly fashion. Several girls were dancing together, which was strictly against the rules. Over near the French doors to the terrace, the row of boys was writhing like a single organism, pinching and jostling, making jokes behind their hands about the poor losers still out on the dance floor, no doubt, while keeping one eye on the fierce-looking chaperones who moved slowly around the room.

As Cecile watched, one of the taller boys suddenly slipped through the door to the terrace and disappeared. "No fair!" she cried.

"What's no fair?" Her partner looked her square in the face for the first time. He was trying hard not to smile, she realized as he shook his fair hair off his forehead. If she wasn't mistaken, he was laughing at her.

"Nothing," she said, lifting her chin. She didn't like being smiled down at like that, as if he were much older. Who did he think he was?

"What? Did Barlow get away?" He swung her effortlessly around so he faced the door; Cecile had to clutch his shoulder to keep from tripping over her feet. "Yep, he got away," he said admiringly. "They're all going to duck out of here before this dog-and-pony show is over."

"How do you know?" Cecile said.

"We do it every year," he said. "Our mothers make us come, and we hate it. I told my mother this was my last year."

"Why do you do it at all?"

"My mother's one of the chaperones."

"Poor you."

He looked at her.

"Sorry." Cecile looked down and grinned before she looked back up. "Do girls ever duck out with them?"

"Girls love this kind of thing."

"Not all girls." Cecile wrenched her hand out of his and stepped back. "Not all girls are the same, you know," she said.

"Okay, okay. Don't get all worked up," he said, pulling her roughly back into the circle of his arm. "It'll cause a scene, and I'll get in trouble if you bite me," he said, picking up where they'd left off. "Have mercy."

"I wasn't going to bite you."

"You looked mean enough to."

They were moving together now, not really dancing; talking was more like it. A couple stumbled past them—the boy's shirttails were pulled out, the girl had a determined frown on her face. "You step on my foot one more time and I'm going to give you a kick you'll never forget," she muttered.

"Most unladylike," Cecile's partner said. "Tsk, tsk."

Cecile laughed. "What do you do after you escape?" she asked.

"Run around . . . look for golf balls on the course to sell to the pro in the morning. Fun stuff."

"You're not supposed to run on the green," said Cecile, who'd been listening to the specific rules of a golf course since she was old enough to understand. "They'd kill you if they found out."

"We take off our shoes. It's the best place to play NMP."

"What's NMP?"

"Nighttime Marco Polo."

"I've never heard of it." Cecile tossed her head, as if her not hearing about it made it less exciting. Because it was exciting; she could feel it.

"You wouldn't have," the boy said. "We made it up."

"How do you play?"

He halted and stared hard at her for a minute, as if sizing up her potential for initiation into a secret club. A club where the members slipped through closed doors and ran around in illegal places, at night. Cecile's heart was racing. She hoped she looked old enough, she hoped she looked worthy, though she didn't know what it took.

"Why? Are you interested?" he asked her at last.

"Maybe." Cecile's eyes were wide and serious.

"Stop looking like that," he said quickly, looking back over his shoulder. "My mother's going to think we're planning a bank robbery."

Cecile changed her expression.

"Now you look like they caught us and you're in jail. Let's dance again for a second." He grabbed her around the waist carelessly and pulled her closer than before, as if some invisible barrier between them had been breached. "Okay," he said, having apparently decided. He looked appraisingly around the dance floor while he talked. "This dance is almost over. When the music stops, the chaperones will start serving refreshments. You walk over to the door while I go talk to my mother. When you get outside, go left and wait for me next to the pillar at the end of the porch."

"What will we do then?"

"Just do it."

The music stopped. Couples around the dance floor quickly dropped their partner's hands, clapped dutifully for a second, and made a mad scramble for the punch table. "Go on," the boy said, giving her a shove.

Cecile walked to the doors on the other side of the room as the rest of the dancers got into line in front of the large tables near the foyer. Her partner went up to the chaperone who'd given them all their instructions at the beginning of the night and grabbed her waist. She turned and put her arm around his shoulder, laughing. Cecile slipped out, onto the terrace.

To her right, the parents who would take their children home after the dance were having dinner in the large screened dining room that overlooked the swimming pool. Cecile heard the familiar shouts of laughter and clinking of glasses as she hurried in the other direction. She stood beside the pillar closest to the path that led to the pro shop and the sixth green.

This was so much more exciting than the dance, she thought as she slipped around to the other side to avoid being seen by two boys who walked quickly by on the path, whispering conspiratorially. Backing into someone standing behind her, she jumped.

"Who'd you think it was, the big, bad boogeyman?" Her dance partner was crouched in the dark; his voice was low and amused. "Take off your shoes and leave them here," he told her, "or they really will kill us tomorrow."

Cecile slipped off her sandals and kicked them beside his shoes. The grass was cool and damp; she rubbed her arms. "Come on," he said, jerking his head. "Let's go."

She followed him away from the clubhouse without talking; he acted as if she weren't there. Hushed voices called softly to one another as they approached the fairway; laughs erupted and were immediately stifled. When they reached the end of the path, Cecile saw dim figures racing about under the moon; something pale was being tossed. "Got it!" called a voice, low and close. "Trevor!"

"Got it!" called the next catcher. "David!"

Cecile and the boy stepped onto the course. The manicured grass under her feet felt like the bristles on a brush. Knowing she shouldn't be on it made her shiver.

"Here's Whit!" called a boy.

"It's about time," called another.

Figures materialized out of the night like spirits and became boys: short boys and tall, with eager, lively faces, hair flopping on foreheads. Some were still wearing their ties, others had taken them off; their unbuttoned white shirts gleamed in the darkness, rising and falling against heaving chests. There wasn't a blue blazer to be seen.

"Who's that with you?" a boy asked suspiciously.

Whit looked at Cecile standing by his side. His eyes met hers; he offered no help.

"Cecile," she said defiantly, emboldened to be standing shoulder to shoulder with their leader.

"Aw, man . . . a girl?" came a voice from the back of the group.

"Who cares?" said another voice. "Let's get going."

"Rules first," Whit said.

The group begrudgingly dismissed Cecile's presence and turned their attention to him. "Two guys are Polo," Whit said. "They get a ten-second start. When we call Marco, they have to call Polo. Then we wait another ten seconds before we call Marco again, right?"

Cecile saw it in her mind's eye: two foxes, hunters on horseback; the thrill of the chase, the chaos in the dark.

"How're we supposed to know ten seconds?" someone growled.

"Don't ask dumb questions," another boy muttered. There was pushing and shoving, a few laughs.

"Boundaries," Whit said in a louder voice. "No leaving the runway or green except to go into the woods behind the cup. You can't go back to the clubhouse or hide behind the pro shop, either."

"Yeah, Michael, no going into the swimming pool like last time," someone called. Murmured agreement.

No. Not foxes and hounds—the Lost Boys, banding together for adventure. Whit was Peter Pan and she was Wendy. But a proud, daring

Wendy, Cecile thought, not a silly little nagger.

The breeze off the bay ruffled her hair. The moon slipped out from behind a wispy cloud and shone down on them before another cloud dimmed it; it lit up their faces. The air smelled of gentle sweat and borrowed aftershave lotion, hopefully splashed. The distant sounds of life on the porch were more memory than real.

"Okay. Let's get going," Whit declared. "The way everyone's bailing out, the chaperones are going to come looking for us in about ten minutes."

"Peter and I will be It." A tall boy with curly hair and his tie dangling around his neck stepped forward with another boy beside him. "No tie pulling and no shirt ripping, either. If I come home from one more dance with a torn shirt, I'm going to catch hell."

"Give us ten seconds," the other boy said.

The two boys melted into the dark.

"One one thousand," a chorus of low voices began. "Two one thousand . . ."

Cecile was filled with the same exhilaration she'd seen in the faces of the boys. It felt almost like panic; her breaths were short and quick. She was determined not to look at Whit, not to make him think she needed him in any way.

"Some of them lie flat on the ground to fool you." Whit's quiet voice in her ear made Cecile start. He grabbed her arm to keep her close. "Watch out. It's easy to trip."

"Ten one thousand. Marco!" the group called in a single, exalted voice.

"Shhh." This from Whit.

Silence. And then, over to the right—farther away than it seemed possible for someone to run in the dark in so short a time—"Polo!" came a taunting, hushed voice.

And a second later, "Polo!" over to their left, near the green.

There was a split second of indecision as the group glanced at one another, deciding which boy to pursue. Then they broke up and ran, some to the left, others to the right. Cecile ran, too, not in any one direction, but zigzagging over the course, following first one figure and then another, as the darting shapes broke apart and came together again. Shouts of "Marco!" and "Polo!" resounded over the dark course, bouncing off the trees lining the fairway, growing carelessly louder as the club fell away and they had the world to themselves.

"Got him! I found Peter!" came a triumphant cry.

"Hank's It!"

"Marco!"

"Polo!"

"Marco!"

There was no way to make sense of it; Cecile felt dizzy with the effort. Panting, she darted over to the line of trees and fell against one. She pushed her hair back off her face and leaned forward with her hands on her knees to catch her breath. It was a good thing she'd taken off that silly bra. Because that's what she had done: at the last minute, when her mother and father were waiting in the car, she'd cried, "Hold on a second!" and run upstairs over Natalie's protests to rip her dress off over her head and unfasten her bra.

The relief had been immediate. Horrible thing's like a tourniquet, Cecile thought as she moved her shoulders now, luxuriating in the delicious freedom of the fabric against her skin. She felt sleek and safe, hiding in the dark—an animal of speed, a spectator on the sidelines of an invisible game until she felt like joining back in. Someone plunged quietly into the trees behind her and swore. A low grunt sounded very near to where she stood, over to the right. There was the sound of heavy breathing. Then a sudden, breathless, "Polo!"

Whit was so close, all she had to do was reach out and touch him. Then she'd be the fox. Everyone would hunt for her. What would it feel like, to be the one the boys were hunting in the dark? To be a fox, outnumbered and surrounded?

Cecile's chest heaved and caught as a hand clamped on her wrist and a voice whispered, "Do you want to be It?"

Whit's breath was warm on her ear. Cecile turned her head. It was too soon, too sudden!

"Not yet," she whispered back.

Whit moved immediately off. She heard him go deeper into the woods, leading the dogs away. She was afraid to breathe.

"Whit! Whit Riley!" A man's heavy, commanding voice rang out over the course. "All of you! Over here now. Please."

If nobody else moved, she wouldn't either. There was no way for the caller to be sure they were out there. If they all stayed quiet, he'd give up and go back to the party.

"Aw, no fair, Mr. Riley!" a boy's voice answered.

There was an immediate chorus of good-natured voices; loud laughter rang out of the trees and bounded carelessly off the green and the fairway; they filled the night. The jig was up. Better luck next year.

Cecile stepped onto the fairway as boys loomed out of the dark all around her; she followed them slowly as they streamed toward the voice. Flocking around the tall, broad-shouldered man in a dinner jacket standing at the end of the path, holding a glass, they fell back to leave an aisle for Whit down the middle as he walked toward his father.

"Hey, Dad," he said, ducking his head to hide his grin.

"Wise guy." Mr. Riley threw his arm around Whit's shoulders and looked around at the sheepish-looking group in front of him. "No wonder your mother's on the warpath. You must have the entire male population of the dance out here. Those poor girls will be frantic."

Poor girls, indeed! Cecile could feel the boys relaxing around her, basking in the maleness of Whit's father. "We're not all poor," she wanted to say and step courageously forward into the light—there was one girl, at least, who wasn't frantic. How dare they!

"Come on, boys, everyone back inside." Mr. Riley turned with his arm still around Whit's shoulder and started back. "They might bite you, but they won't eat you," he called over his shoulder consolingly, "and it's almost over."

The boys fell in behind them, grousing as they stooped to snatch blazers from the ground, to smooth hair back from hot foreheads and exchange triumphant grins: a herd of male animals, bonded by their shared fate. Cecile was all but forgotten.

Silly boys, she thought as she trailed behind them. She couldn't resent them, it had been too much fun. She'd never tell anyone about this, not a soul.

"Believe it or not," she heard Whit's father say, "but one of these days, I won't be able to pry you boys away from the same girls with a crowbar."

"No way!" a few boys yelled, and Mr. Riley laughed. The group broke up when they reached the terrace, each boy going in search of his shoes. Cecile waited until Whit's father had joined the rest of the parents on the porch before she went over to the pillar where she'd left her shoes. Whit was there, putting on his.

"Go around to the front door and come in that way," he said, giving her a dismissive glance. "If my mother sees I brought a girl out here, I'll really catch it." He stood up and straightened his tie, looking down at her coolly as she knelt to put on her sandals.

It was gone, all gone! She was nothing but a bur-
den now. "You're not the boss of me," Cecile said,
tucking her hair behind her ears as she stood back
up. He gave a short, amused laugh as she twirled and
walked away.

So what if she'd sounded more like Lucy than a
twelve-year-old? She'd made Whit laugh, hadn't she?
It was a good kind of laugh, too. An amused laugh,
not an "I'm only doing this to make you think
you're funny" laugh. He'd liked her enough to invite
her to run around barefoot in the dark, too, and play
a game with a bunch of boys.

Next time, she'd be ready.

Headlights swept across the path from the steady
stream of cars pulling into the driveway in front of
the club. Cecile leaned against the lattice, covered
with vines, that lined the path to adjust her sandal.
Somewhere ahead of her, a boy laughed. It sounded as
if it came from the small space that had been cut
into the privet hedge for a curved stone bench.

Cecile knew it well. It was where they used to
hide when the family was on their way back to the

car. The children would run ahead and duck into the space to hide and then leap out, shouting, when Mr. and Mrs. Thompson drew near. She wondered if some of the boys from the course were hiding there now, hoping to scare her.

It was Natalie. She darted out of the space as if she were being pursued and was immediately followed by William. He grabbed Natalie's arm and whipped her around, pulling her against him as he wrapped his arms around her back so she couldn't get away. Natalie didn't even try. She stood on tiptoe with her hands against William's chest and kissed him.

Oh, ugh. And on the mouth, too. Was that what all the hair tossing and fake laughter had been about, so she could kiss a boy with fat lips?

Natalie and William broke apart and started walking toward the waiting cars. By the time Cecile came around the corner of the club, William was nowhere to be seen and Natalie was standing beside their mother in a group of parents near the front door. Groups of girls ran down the steps past them and climbed into the backseats of cars. A few boys whose faces Cecile thought she recognized stood in a clump off to one side.

Natalie caught Cecile's eye as she walked up to them and asked, "How long were you back there?"

"Long enough."

Natalie's eyes flashed, quick and telegraphic, like their mother's smile.

"Your father's gone to get the car," Mrs. Thompson said as she bent to smooth Cecile's dress where it had caught up on one side. "Did you have fun? How'd the dancing go?"

"Okay."

"Come and say thank you to Mrs. Riley," Mrs. Thompson said as she led them over to Whit's harried-looking mother, who was standing in the foyer, saying her good-byes. "My daughters want to tell you what a wonderful time they had, Nina," their mother said.

"Thank you," Cecile said. "I had a wonderful time."

"Thanks. It was spectacular." Natalie flashed her smile.

"What charming daughters you have, Anne." Mrs. Riley looked at them with vague eyes, as if unsure who they were. They could have been any of the girls she'd been in charge of that night. "And what charming Peonys. I do hope Whit had a chance to dance with you both."

The girls entered their bedroom quietly so as not to wake Lucy. Cecile stepped out of her dress and dropped it on the bottom of her bed, then crawled under her sheets. They smelled of sunshine and fresh air. Sheba must have changed them during the day.

She listened to the sounds of Natalie in the bathroom: the heavy thunk of the cabinet door, water gushing into the sink, the flush of the toilet. After what felt like ages, Natalie opened the door and switched off the light. The bedroom was thrown into darkness.

"How could you?" Cecile said when she heard Natalie's bed creak as she got into it.

"How could I what?" Natalie said, yawning.

"Kiss William."

"I knew you were spying on us."

"I was not." Indignation made Cecile sit up. "If you really want to know, I was on the golf course, running around with a bunch of boys."

"What boys?"

"None of your business."

"Yeah, right, Cecile."

Cecile lay back down. Neither one of them said anything for a minute. Then, "He has slobbery lips," Cecile said. "I don't see how you can stand it."

"What's the big deal?" Natalie said. "It's only practice."

"Practice for what?"

"You don't think you wait until you meet the boy of your dreams and then immediately start mashing with him, do you? The last thing you want is for a boy you like to think you don't know what you're doing."

Why not? Cecile wanted to ask. How can you kiss a boy you don't even like? "I think it's disgusting," she said stubbornly.

"Fine. Do what you want." She could tell that Natalie had rolled over and was facing the window.

"I don't think you have to worry about it anytime soon, anyway."

That's all you know, Cecile thought. She'd rather be chased in the dark, any day, than kiss a boy with slobbery lips on the mouth. Cecile couldn't even remember what Whit's mouth looked like. All she could remember was the strange way the hairs on her arm had stood up when she felt his warm breath in her ear.

Chapter Twelve

"Don't tell me you turned into a teenager after one dance." Sheba looked up from the sink where she was holding the huge bowl she'd mixed muffins in when Cecile came into the kitchen the next morning and smiled.

"What do you mean?"

"It's eight thirty. You missed Jack by a long shot this morning. Did you have a good time?"

"It was okay. Can I have a muffin?" Cecile put her face close to the muffin tin Sheba had just taken out of the oven and breathed deep. "Mmm, blueberry."

"Take one for Jack, too," Sheba said as Cecile carefully checked them all and selected the one with the most blueberries oozing their dark juice.

"Unless you're not going down to the dock straight-away this morning."

"Of course I am. Ouch!" Cecile held the muffin she'd bitten into away from her mouth as a swirl of trapped heat curled up.

"You know those things are hot," Sheba said. "How many times have you been burned?"

"A million." Cecile took the muffin Sheba had wrapped in a napkin for Jack and headed for the back door.

"Is that all you're going to tell me about last night?" Sheba said.

"Umm . . ." Cecile held open the screen door while she thought. "Boys have sweaty hands, chaper-ones are like wolves . . . and dances are dumb." She let the door slam behind her. "Bye!"

She cut across the lawn, onto the drive. The muf-fin was still warm in her hand when she reached the dock. Jack and Leo were sitting side by side on the float in their matching orange life vests.

"Are those your feet I see in the water?" she called as she walked down the dock.

"King's here."

"Where? I don't see him."

"In the boathouse, fixing an engine." Jack said something quiet to Leo. They quickly lifted their feet out of the water and stood up as Cecile came down the ramp. "I saw you coming," Jack said. "And I can swim as well as you and Natalie."

"That's not the point. What about Leo? Here." Cecile handed Jack the muffin. "I didn't know Leo was here, so I only have one."

"We'll split it," Jack said.

"For the last time." Leo said, turning his mournful, pale face to Cecile. Other than a sprinkling of bright freckles over his nose and cheeks, it showed no signs of his having spent the past week in the sun.

"What's wrong with you?" said Cecile.

"He has to go home tomorrow," said Jack.

"Right. I forgot. Oh, well," Cecile said carelessly, only halfway through her vacation. "Maybe you'll come back next year."

That meant Jenny was leaving tomorrow, too.

Even that thought didn't dampen her spirits. She liked the idea of being alone again. She might go to the club with her mother, or she might not. She could do anything she wanted.

"Hello! Anybody out there?"

"King?" Cecile said. She slowly approached the boathouse doors and peered into its murky depths, strangely shy. Her eyes adjusted slowly to the dim light.

"Cecile, wonderful! I need your help. I'm trying to fix this blasted thing."

King was kneeling in a far corner in front of a small engine he'd apparently taken apart and which was now scattered in pieces around him on the cement floor.

"Stefan couldn't get the dinghy started yesterday," King told her as she came up to him. "I'm trying to see what the problem is."

"Who's Stefan?" Cecile said.

"The cabin boy," King said, glancing up at her. "Actually," he added as if he'd just recognized it, "at seventeen, I suppose we should call him the cabin young man, shouldn't we? And a very competent cabin young man he is, at that."

Stefan. So that was his name.

"You're young and agile. Crawl under there and see if you can find the screwdriver, would you?" King said, gesturing toward the low bench against the wall. "I can't see a damned thing with my eyes."

Cecile crouched down and felt around underneath the bench. "You mean this?" she asked, holding up a tool.

"Perfect. Thank you." King started unscrewing a screw from the engine. "How was your dance, Cinderella? Did you make it home before midnight?"

"It wasn't my dance."

"I trust you weren't part of the bunch that made a mess on the golf course," King said, rifling through the toolbox beside him. "I hear the pro was fit to be tied this morning."

"What kind of mess?" Her father would kill her.

"They tore up the sixth green a bit. Apparently someone pulled out the flag and tossed it into the woods. That kind of thing."

So that was what the boys had been throwing between them when she and Whit arrived. "You think I'd run on a green, with *my* father?" Cecile said.

"Right. You're a seasoned little golf orphan, aren't you?" King sat back on his haunches and looked at her. "I'm sure it was the boys. Boys have been ducking out of those dances since I was forced to go to them. Are they still as torturous as they used to be, or are you one of those girls who likes dances?"

"I think they're silly," Cecile said. "How'd you know it wasn't girls running around on the course?"

"That's the spirit, Heathen. When you start liking dances, I'll know it's time to throw in the towel."

She stood watching King in silence for a minute. "How come you know so much about engines?" she said at last. "You're a lawyer."

"Lawyers do know one or two things besides law," King said, tinkering with the engine again. "My father made me take apart and rebuild the engines of more of his cars than I like to remember."

"Oh," Cecile said. Then, nonchalantly, "What does it mean when a boy says a girl is too much work?"

"Ha!" King glanced up at her. "Where'd you hear that?"

"I don't know." Cecile shrugged. "The dance?"

"You certainly were around a bunch who're going to grow up to be a lot of work, in that crowd."

Cecile slung her arm around one of the poles that held up the roof and leaned away from it like a flag at half mast. "So, what does it mean?"

"It means she's demanding. Costly to maintain," said King. "Our old Bentley is too much work. I'm still paying the earth to keep it on the road and it's old enough to be my father." King looked up as Cecile circled the pole slowly with it nestled in the crook of her arm and said, "That pole's riddled with splinters. Creosote-covered ones."

Cecile stopped and brushed the skin on the inside of her elbow as she said, "So it's an insult."

"I guess it is," said King. "But as you will come

to find out, Cecile, if you haven't already, many girls like expensive jewelry and clothing. When they grow up, their husbands have to pay for manicures and hairdressers and a grand house. It adds up, let me tell you."

"I'll never be like that," Cecile said. "I don't even like jewelry."

"No, I don't think you will." King tossed the screwdriver into the toolbox and stood up, smiling at her as he brushed off the knees of his slacks. "It's a good thing, too. As successful as your father is, no man should have to support four demanding women in one family."

"Four?" Cecile said, counting quickly. "You mean Lucy?" she said, amazed. "You can already tell about *Lucy*?"

"I wouldn't be at all surprised." King tousled her hair as he went past her, heading for the door. "I have to find Mr. Peabody and enlist his help with this blasted thing. Just keep your sense of humor," he said as Cecile followed him out into the sun. "Boys like a girl with a sense of humor."

"Not all boys!" Cecile shouted as King bounded up the steps.

"The ones worth running after do," he called. "Bye, Heathen."

Jenny was as droopy as Leo when she came down to the dock. She didn't want to get wet, she said, because she'd only have to dry off, and she insisted on wearing her sandals on the beach. "What's the point?" she said. "I'm not going to walk barefoot in New York City."

The only interest she showed in the dance was to ask, "Was it horrible?" When Cecile told her about the first boy she danced with, Jenny said, "I told you to wear a back shield," in an unsympathetic voice.

"One of them wasn't too bad," Cecile said.

"I'm going to a party tonight, but it's for families."

"You'll have to dance with Leo."

"Don't make me barf."

It was a listless sort of morning. A chasm had opened up between them, with the person who was staying on one side against the person who was leaving on the other; there seemed to be no common language. They searched the pools on the rocks for a while, but there wasn't any excitement in it. Jenny finally had to go home so her mother could curl her hair and spray it. Cecile walked with her up the drive, picturing Jenny in huge pink rollers and afterward, her straight hair marked with ridges.

"Hair spray's for old ladies," Cecile told her.

"The curls will fall out in about ten seconds if I don't," Jenny said fussily. For the briefest second, she looked like her mother.

Cecile was happy to go back to the house when they parted at the cottage. She stood in the front hall and listened for sounds of life, but it was quiet. Everyone must still be at the club. She went onto the terrace and lay down on Granddad's chaise under the awning.

The rest of the terrace was baking in the hot sun. Someone had put a vase of roses under the umbrella on the glass-topped table. The striped mallets from the croquet set their father had set up on the lawn stood ready and waiting in their cart. So this is what the day after a party feels like, Cecile thought contentedly as she stretched her legs and wiggled her toes. Maybe she would go upstairs to borrow some of her mother's nail polish. No, she'd only have to take it off.

She heard voices in the living room. "Who goes there?" Cecile called.

There was a silence before her father opened the screen door and stuck his head out. "What're you doing out here all by yourself?"

"Not much." Cecile craned around. "Who's with you?"

"Everyone. Mom and Natalie went upstairs, and Lucy and Jack are in the kitchen, begging. I'm going up to change." The door started to swing shut as her father stepped back into the living room. "By the way," he said, sticking his head out again. "I have a message for you."

"From who?"

"Whit Riley."

Cecile sat up and swung around to face him with such a surprised expression on her face that her father laughed. "How do you know Whit?" he said.

Cecile shrugged. "He was one of the boys I danced with. What'd he say?"

"It was very cryptic." Her father looked amused. "He said, 'Tell Cecile NMP at eight o'clock tonight.' You two aren't spies, by any chance?"

"NMP?" Cecile said, working to keep her face blank. "What's that supposed to mean?"

"If you don't know, I don't know," her father said. "Whit's a nice boy. Anyway, that's the message."

He let the door slam behind him this time. Cecile lay back down. Nighttime Marco Polo. Whit, inviting her. But how could she get to the club tonight when they'd been there last night? Her parents would never let her go by herself. Maybe she could talk Natalie into it and they could convince the whole family to go. They could say they wanted to have dinner and swim in the pool after dark. Cecile could slip away and join the game. In her bathing suit, yet! Wouldn't they be surprised.

Imagining the soft night air whispering against her skin as she ran and hid, Cecile shivered. The breath of the panting boys as they chased her would be warm on her neck if she were caught. Then would come the grip of a hand on her arm—

When the screen door slammed, Cecile sat up guiltily. "Granddad's about to come down, Cecile," her mother said. "Get up from his chair, would you?"

Her mother's dark hair was slicked back from her forehead, her face more beautiful for being without makeup. Her sleeveless white dress, falling in elegant folds, was as simple as a sack. A white headband dangled around her neck like a necklace. "Hungry?" she asked invitingly, holding out a platter of cheese and crackers.

"Thanks." Cecile got up off the chaise and took a piece of cheese. Her mother put the platter on the table and sat down. "What'd you do today?" she asked, girlishly pulling up her legs to rest her heels on the edge of her seat. The polish on her toenails was the faintest pink; even her narrow feet were beautiful.

She looked happy and relaxed; it was the perfect time to ask.

Cecile sat down next to her. "Nothing much," she said. "I fooled around with Jenny, but it wasn't much fun. Jenny's depressed because they're leaving tomorrow. So's Leo."

"It's been nice for you having her here, hasn't it?"

"It's been okay. It'll be nice having the Island to ourselves again." Cecile took another piece of cheese. "Where's Natalie?" she asked.

"Upstairs taking a shower." Her mother was tousling her wet hair with one hand. "She's going to a party tonight with William."

Perfect.

"Really? Then can I go to the club after dinner for a while?" Cecile leaned forward. "A bunch of kids I know will be there."

"Tonight?" Her mother sounded surprised. "You've never wanted to go to the club at night before. What kids?"

"Just some I met at the dance. They're playing a game."

"Oh. Well, not tonight. One late night in a weekend is enough at your age."

"That's not fair. How come Natalie can go out two nights in a row, and I can't?"

"I wasn't going to let her, but William's mother put in a word for her." Her mother tucked a few stray hairs behind her ears. "Mr. and Mrs. Cahoon are going to be at the same party and Mrs. Cahoon asked because it's William's last night."

"I don't see why I can't go if Natalie can."

"Because I said no."

"You wouldn't let her go if you knew the things she and William have been doing together," Cecile said.

"Cecile Thompson." Her mother stopped preening and frowned. "You sound like a little prude," she said coldly.

Her mother meant for it to sting. Cecile felt the unfairness of it in the tightness of her throat.

"For one thing, Natalie's almost fifteen and you're twelve," her mother said. "For another thing, Granddad, Dad, and I are going to the Whites' for dinner. We are not leaving you at the club, on your own, at night, and that's final."

"You get to go out. And I won't be alone. Other people will be there."

"Stop it." Her mother was done talking. "You can go another night, unless you keep at it, and then you can't go at all."

"There may not *be* another night!"

It could have been Natalie speaking; her mother was as shocked as Cecile. If it hadn't been for Granddad coming onto the terrace, Cecile didn't know what either one of them would have said next.

"Well, well, well . . . what have we here?" Granddad said as he came toward them, resplendent in a madras jacket, white pants, and red bow tie, and rested his hand on the top of Cecile's head. "Am I interrupting something?" he asked, looking into his daughter's dissatisfied face.

"Of course not, Dad. Everything's fine." Her mother's face cleared; she smiled up at him. "Cecile was asking if she could go to the club tonight and I told her we're going out to dinner, so she can't. Cecile understands she'll have to go another night, right, Cecile?"

Cecile returned her mother's level look. "Right," she said.

Her mother's brow became as smooth and clear as a baby's. "Run and tell Sheba we're ready for cocktails, that's a good girl," she said. She put her hand over her father's where he'd rested it on her shoulder and nuzzled it with her chin. "You might want to help her by bringing out the ice bucket," she called as Cecile opened the screen door.

And I might not. Cecile let the door swing noisily shut. Everything wasn't fine, either. Just because her mother wanted it to be that way didn't mean that it was. Not this time, she thought as she went past the kitchen and up the stairs to her room. Maybe never again.

Chapter Thirteen

The movie she was watching ended. Cecile got up from the couch, turned off the TV, and walked into the front hall. "I'm going to the dock!" she called in a hushed voice.

The door of the upstairs study opened quietly. Sheba leaned over the banister and looked down.

"You are, huh?"

Cecile couldn't read the expression on Sheba's dark face. "It's only nine o'clock," she said. "The *Rammer* came in before dinner. There'll be plenty of people there, maybe even King. I want to see what's going on."

"You've been seeing what's going on all day long."

Sheba's quiet watchfulness grated on Cecile's

nerves. "Mom would let me," she said defensively. "I won't go anywhere else."

"I never thought you would, but I'm gonna hold you to that." Sheba straightened up and turned back toward the study where she was reading a book to Jack.

What's the big deal? Cecile thought, challenging her reflection in the mirror over the table. All I'm doing is going to the dock.

Two limousines were waiting in the parking area. The dock was lit up for a party, tiny lights on wires, looped between the pilings. Music from the *Rammer* floated over the water. Cecile climbed onto a piling near the boathouse to watch.

Everyone was at a party except her. And Lucy and Jack, and they were babies. Cecile took a strand of hair and chewed on the end, watching as women in colorful summer dresses threw back their heads and laughed and men with tanned faces slouched as they talked, their drinks conveniently replenished by a bartender who came up from the cabin, again and again.

It was too much to expect that she would be content to sit, all night, and do nothing. Not when the music was making her blood dance in time to the reflection of the lights sparkling on the water. I may not be fourteen, Cecile told herself as she jumped back off the piling, but I'm not a baby, either.

At the sound of footsteps, she turned. Stefan was coming toward her carrying a tray. He wore a white shirt, black pants, and a black bow tie. His long hair shone under the lanterns that had been placed on top of the tall poles lining the dock.

"Hello, *Ste*fan," Cecile said, leaning on his name, daring and reckless.

He looked at her without a spark of recognition. Insulted, she refused to back down. He *had* to say something to her—they were the only two people here, and Cecile lived on the Island while he worked for King. The bare truth of it shocked her. She lifted her chin, defiant and proud.

Then another voice called out from near the cabanas, another imperious voice, and Cecile felt ashamed.

"Where have you *been*? I've been looking all over for you." A tall, large-boned blond woman wearing very high heels teetered toward them. Sparkling earrings drooped from her ears; her mouth was scarlet, her teeth white, her dress cut so low, Cecile saw the white line of her tan across generous cleavage.

"I'd about given up on you," the woman said as she came up to Stefan. "As soon as we finish our cocktails, we're going into town. Mmm . . . these look luscious." Putting a hand on Stefan's shoulder, she moved her other hand in the air above the hors d'oeuvres, trying to make up her mind. Her hand dropped and two perfectly manicured fingers, like the talons of a hawk, closed around a stuffed clam. She bit into it, smiling into Stefan's face as she chewed.

Cecile could have reached out and touched them, she was so close; the woman never even looked at her. The woman licked one finger and then the other before she said, "We'd better go before I eat them all," and she and Stefan turned and walked toward the *Rammer*, the woman keeping her hand on Stefan's shoulder as they walked. Cecile willed Stefan to turn around and look at her, but he didn't.

Luscious, she mouthed cattily; she stuck out her tongue. And you, Stefan, letting a woman make eyes at you when she's old enough to be your mother. Fine. Cecile's mind was made up with a toss of her head. Since no one cares that I'm here, I'll go someplace where they do care.

The idea must have been lurking in the back of her mind all night. It burst into flame and blazed as bright and clear as a bonfire as she ran up the steps. She knew the way, she would walk. Down the driveway, turn right, along the road half a mile, turn left at the pillared entrance. So what if there were no street lights? She'd driven the road a million times.

She flitted past Granddad's house with its front porch lit up by huge lanterns, skimmed past the driveways to the cottage and the caretaker's house, and arrived at the straightaway to the bridge. It stretched ahead of her like a shiny ribbon in the light of the half moon, calling, Follow me, follow me! Cecile was surprised to discover she was breathing heavily.

She walked along the bridge slowly until she got to the middle and leaned over the railing. The breeze was warm on her face. Sparks ricocheted off the surface of the water as it gurgled under her feet. The sharp smell of salt water seemed thick enough to eat.

How strange, to be in this spot, by herself, at night. It had never happened to her before. There were no streetlights lining the road, no other houses showing their lights through the trees. No human sounds disturbed the silence, not even those she knew were being made at the dock. There was only the wind in her ears and the ripple of the water under the bridge.

The road to the club was dark. Cecile imagined the feel of it under her bare feet; the grass on the golf course would be damp and cold. How amazing it would be, to slip onto the green without the boys seeing her and join in the game, unannounced. Imagine the shock for the first boy who put his hands on her.

The breeze was suddenly cool. Cecile shivered and

rubbed her arms, thinking about the long walk back. The dark road would be black by then; the driveway, silent and lonely. What if her parents were waiting for her, stony-faced, in the front hall? What then? Or even worse, what if the house itself was dark, the doors securely locked, everyone blissfully asleep in their beds, believing that Cecile was asleep, too, safe and warm.

Cecile looked back. The flag was still up in front of the house. The spotlight on the pole in front of Granddad's house showed it drooping by itself in the night. Forgotten.

That never would have happened when they were little. They'd all begged to be the one to take it down every night. Granddad had had to make a rule that they'd rotate in order from the oldest to the youngest. Now nobody seemed to care except for Jack, who needed help to do it. Even Cecile had only taken it down once in all the days they'd been here.

She still cared, even if no one else did. She'd go back and take the flag down, fold it the proper way, and then go into the house and find something good to eat. Maybe she'd curl up on the couch and watch TV until Natalie came home. "Marco! Polo!" she called softly as she walked back up the drive. "Marco!"

A car coming around the corner on the bay road made a wet swishing sound. It slowed as it approached the island and suddenly turned, its headlights sweeping across the drive to light up the bridge. Cecile leaped into the grass and ducked down as the car's tires rumbled on the wooden slats. When it rolled slowly past, she saw Natalie in the front seat, looking straight ahead. She heard the rhythmic thump of music.

Cecile stayed crouched until the car disappeared around the curve and then stood up slowly. She couldn't go right back now—she'd have to give William time to walk Natalie to the door and give her a good-night kiss—yuck—before he'd finally, finally go home. Forever, she thought. Tomorrow, they'd have the Island back to themselves, at last! She could wait.

She took her time, identifying constellations, as she wandered up the drive, receiving a small shock as she rounded the corner—the Cahoons' car was parked in Mr. Peabody's driveway. Its engine and lights were turned off; the murmur of voices came from inside.

Tense as a wild animal who suddenly encounters humans, wary to think what Natalie and William might be doing inside, Cecile started to walk skittishly past when the car abruptly shook. Cecile couldn't see their heads, but she heard Natalie's laugh and William's low voice. Then all was quiet again.

When headlights coming from the dock suddenly lit up the drive, Cecile was caught once again. She darted onto the grass, but not before she saw William's and Natalie's heads pop up in the backseat, the headlights of the limousines lighting up their startled faces as the cars slid past.

Then the limousines disappeared around the corner and the world was plunged back into dark. "William, no!" she heard Natalie cry. Then a growl from William and Natalie's laugh.

How she hated them. William, sounding like an animal, and her own sister willing to lie on the seat of a car and kiss a boy she didn't even care about, as if she was anybody; any silly girl in the world who kissed a boy, no matter how disgusting, just so she could say she'd made out.

And on Gull Island, too.

Cecile picked up a handful of shells and gravel and hurled it. The sound of the pieces rattling against the roof and the windows of the car sounded in her ears as she ran up the drive. Her mother had called her a prude. Fine. She'd rather be a prude than be like Natalie. Or even her mother, flirting to make her own husband mad. Cecile's stomach and lungs felt as if they were on fire as she ran, but her mind was as cold as ice. It was a good cold; it made it easier for her brain to think.

So what if Natalie and her mother were pretty? That didn't make them more special than every other girl in the world, did it? Any girl could get a boy to pay attention to her. Cecile could herself. It all depended on what the boy wanted.

No. Not what the boy wanted, what the girl wanted. What she, Cecile, wanted. What she wanted right now, here, this very instant, was to show the world what she thought of it. She didn't know what she was going to do, or how she was going to do it, but she was confident it would come to her.

A deep quiet and total darkness, except for a single strand of lights still sparkling on the bow of the *Rammer*, greeted her when she reached the steps. The dim security lights set low on the pilings were the only other light. They cast eerie shadows the length of the dock.

Cecile walked slowly down to the dock, letting her hand drag along the railing until she heard a low cough, and then she stopped. Stefan was perched on the stern of the *Rammer*, watching her. His legs dangled over the edge of the boat, his bow tie was stuffed into the pocket of his shirt. He was smoking; the tip of his cigarette lit up his face when he inhaled. He paused, then let a thin curl of smoke escape his mouth to drift up in front of his face.

Maybe because it was dark, or maybe because it was just the two of them, but Cecile wasn't afraid. She walked to the middle of the dock, in front of the cabanas, and put her hands on her hips. She stared at him, good and hard for a minute, so he would know she saw him.

Then she began.

"Go back . . . go back . . . go back into the woods," she said quietly. She crossed her arms in front of her body and took a step back. "'Cause you haven't"—a slow slash with her arms—"you haven't"—another slash—"you haven't got the goods," she said louder.

Stefan was still, the cigarette held frozen between his thumb and forefinger in front of his mouth as he watched her.

"Now you may have the spirit and you may have the *pep*," Cecile said in a loud voice, "but you haven't got the team that the blue team's got!" She was shouting by the last words, feeling them in her gut, and then she was finished and her heart was racing and her spirits were soaring because Stefan had laughed, and inside, she was laughing, too, and then she ran. Up the steps, over the gravel, along the hedge and across the stinging grass, past the sleeping flag, and into the front hall, pausing only to catch the screen door so it would close silently behind her.

She flew up the stairs and opened the door to her room. She shut it softly behind her and threw herself on her bed. Her chest was heaving as she stared up at the ceiling, her face was split by a wide grin. I can't believe you did that! her heart sang. That was so ridiculous!

Maybe so, her head said calmly when her pulse had slowed enough so that it could be heard. At least now, Stefan had seen her, really seen her, enough to be able to pick her out of a crowd of rich children on the beach.

Cecile woke to the sound of someone being sick in their bathroom. A sliver of light gleamed under the door.

"Natalie?" Cecile whispered, resting her forehead against the door. "Are you all right?"

When Natalie moaned, Cecile pushed the door open. Natalie knelt in front of the toilet with her forearms resting on the rim, her face bent over the bowl. Her hair fell around her face, dank and damp. Her body heaved, she gagged.

"What happened? What'd you do?" Cecile grabbed a washcloth and ran it under cold water. Crouching down, she held it to Natalie's forehead the way her mother did when she was sick. Natalie put her hand to it to hold it and moaned. Cecile smelled a heavy, medicinal smell and stood up.

"So much for being drunk," she said. "Sob, sob."

"Cecile, don't," Natalie groaned. She dropped the washcloth onto the floor and rose up on her knees to put her face over the bowl again. Cecile picked up the cloth and rinsed it under cold water slowly and carefully, listening to her sister being sick.

When Natalie finally sat back and looked up, tears were running along her nose; her damp hair was plastered to her face. "Oh, Natalie," Cecile said, and sank to her knees. She wiped Natalie's hair away from her forehead and cheeks and neck. When Natalie rose up to be sick again, Cecile rinsed the cloth for a third time and stood waiting.

"Oh, God," Natalie moaned as she sagged against

the bathroom wall. "You have no idea how horrible I feel."

"I thought it was what you wanted."

"Don't be mean." Natalie's face when she looked up was so pale, the dark circles under her dull eyes so dark.

"You're an idiot," Cecile said more gently.

"Don't remind me." Natalie closed her eyes and let her head fall back against the wall. "That was you who threw the rocks at the car, wasn't it?" she said, her eyes closed.

"They were tiny pebbles."

"We almost had a heart attack. William was furious. He thought you might have cracked the windshield." Natalie wiped her face with the washcloth. "This is all his fault, the pig."

"You led him on."

"Girls? Are you in there?"

Cecile quickly slipped through the door and shut it behind her as their mother opened their bedroom door and peered in.

"I thought I heard you," her mother said in a low

voice as she glanced at the bathroom. "Is everything all right?"

Cecile stepped into the hall, pulling the bedroom door closed behind her. She leaned against it with her hand on the knob. "Natalie was just telling me about her party," she said. "I was sound asleep, but she had to wake me up to tell me what a wonderful time she had. You know Natalie."

"I certainly do." Her mother yawned as she reached up to take the combs out of her hair. It cascaded around her shoulders, hiding the strand of pearls that lay heavily along her delicate collarbone. "You'll know how it feels someday, too," she told Cecile with a lazy smile. "Someday soon, by the look of it." She lightly kissed Cecile's cheek. "Go to sleep now, it's late."

"Did you have fun at dinner?" Cecile called quietly to her mother's retreating back.

"It was great." Her mother stopped at her bedroom door. "I'll tell you all about it in the morning. Night."

"Night."

Natalie was asleep. A faint sour smell rose up from where she lay in her bed. Cecile crawled under her own sheets and stared up into the dark. Someone closed the heavy front door. The lamps on the front porch were turned out. Slow steps sounded on the stairs, doors quietly closed, the house became still and dark. Nothing more would happen here tonight.

Chapter Fourteen

The morning air was crisp and clear, the blue sky dotted with puffy clouds like dabs of whipped cream, a stiff breeze off the bay promising to blow away all humidity. The water sparkled; the flags on the back of the *Rammer* snapped jauntily in the wind. The high tide that had cleared the beach of all debris now lay lapping lazily against the clean sand. It was a brand-new day.

Poor Jenny, Cecile thought as she headed back up to the house to see what Sheba had made for breakfast. What a horrible day to have to leave. She'd promised to meet Jenny inside the lilac bush at ten o'clock. Maybe one of Sheba's muffins would cheer her up.

"There you are!" her mother called cheerfully when Cecile stood at the screen door to the terrace.

"Come out here! Dad and I have a surprise."

Cecile cautiously pushed the door open. From the sound of her voice, they must have declared a truce. Lucy was snuggled in her mother's lap, her father was sitting at her side. "Guess who's arriving on Thursday?" her mother said happily as she slid her bare feet under his thighs. He patted her ankle, smiling indulgently.

"Who?" Cecile said.

"Harry!" Lucy jiggled up and down in their mother's lap with excitement. "Harry's coming," she cried.

"He is?" Cecile looked from her mother's radiant face to her father's satisfied smile. "How'd that happen?"

"Dad and King worked it out." Her mother's eyes glowed, her smile included the whole world. "Well, Dad worked it out," she said, leaning out to put her slim hand on her husband's cheek, "but with King's encouragement, right, Drew?"

"Your mother wouldn't rest until Harry joined us," he said. "You know what a mother hen she is. I sent a telegram to his employers saying we needed Harry at home."

"We do need him at home." Her mother settled back contentedly. "It hasn't been the same, not having him here, has it, Cecile?"

It hadn't been the same, no. "But I've been having fun," Cecile said.

"Oh, pooh to you." Nothing could dampen her mother's spirits. She was dazzling in her victory. She wrapped her arms more tightly around Lucy and noisily kissed her head all over, making Lucy giggle. "At least Lucy's on my side. You missed Harry, didn't you, baby?"

"No," said Lucy, pretending, which made Mrs. Thompson kiss her more.

"Anyway," Mr. Thompson said to Cecile when he could tear his eyes away from the happy picture of his wife and child, "your mother and I will pick Harry up at the airport on Thursday afternoon and bring him back here for a party."

"A welcome-home party," shouted Lucy. "With balloons and cake!"

Her parents looked so self-satisfied, it would have been bad manners for Cecile not to join in. "Have you told Natalie?" she said.

"That sleepyhead?" Her mother laughed. "We won't see her until noon."

"If we're lucky," her father added.

The mere suggestion of a frown creased her mother's lovely brow. "Cecile, say you're happy," she said. "You're ruining all my fun with that disapproving face."

"I'm happy. I've got to meet Jenny now. She's leaving today."

"Poor Jenny," Mrs. Thompson said with a careless shrug. "Maybe they'll come back next year."

King was driving past when Cecile reached the lilac. He stopped the car and leaned out, smiling as he said, "I hear there's cause for much celebration in the Thompson household."

Cecile walked slowly to the car. "You talked my father into it, didn't you?" she said, refusing to smile. "Because my mother always gets what she wants. Even if it means flirting with you to make him jealous."

King looked at his hands on the steering wheel for a minute and then back at Cecile. His face was kind. "You will learn, as you get older, Cecile, that there are people in this world who can make life miserable for everyone around them if they're not happy, and that it sometimes is a greater show of wisdom if you can help them get what they want for the good of the whole."

"Give in, you mean."

"Ahhh . . ." King rubbed his hand over his chin and mouth as he thought. "Children should try not to be too judgmental as they grow up," he said at last. "Especially not of their elders. There are things at work they can't understand." He gave a small nod of his head. "Although you certainly have a right to your opinion."

"I'm not a child, and I certainly do."

The stiff way she said it made King laugh. It was a real laugh, not a condescending adult's laugh. "Right," he said, slapping his hand on the steering wheel before he put the car into gear. "I will never make that mistake again. You're a tough one, Cecile Thompson, I'll give you that. You might be happier if you can think of it as taking back August. Your father and I took it back, and now," King said, holding out his hand, palm up, like an offering, "I gladly give it to you."

It wasn't his fault. It wasn't anybody's fault. "Very well," Cecile said haughtily, pretending to snatch it. "But next time, I'll want something more expensive."

"A diamond necklace, I promise!"

She grinned to hear King laugh as he pulled away. Then she spun around, arms out, face to the sky. It really was a beautiful day, and she, for one, wasn't leaving. She settled herself inside the lilac bush to wait for Jenny. They were going to decide what to do with Jenny's last morning. Cecile put two of Sheba's warm sticky buns, nestled in a napkin, on a stump.

She'd go along with whatever Jenny wanted to do, she decided. Go swimming, maybe, or look for shells? But when Jenny arrived, it was obvious she wasn't prepared to do either one of these. She wore a starched smocked dress with a round collar and puffed sleeves. And shoes with socks.

Lucy wore smocked dresses, for heaven's sake. Cecile watched with amazement as Jenny smoothed her dress around her as she sat carefully down.

"We're stopping at my grandmother's house for dinner on the way home," Jenny explained primly when she was finally settled. She adjusted her velvet headband in case it had slipped. "I had to get dressed so my mother can pack up everything."

"Here," Cecile said, holding out the napkin. "I brought you a sticky bun."

"I already brushed my teeth."

"More for me then, I guess," Cecile said.

She eyed Jenny warily while she ate. Jenny looked so odd, sitting there. It was as if one minute, she'd been sitting in a church pew, and the next, she'd been magically transported here, swept up by Dorothy's tornado, maybe, to end up sitting on a stump inside a bush. All she lacked were white gloves.

"There's not too much you can do this morning, dressed like that," Cecile said.

"I know."

Jenny patted her hair and smoothed her dress again. She looked important and self-conscious, as if she were the keeper of a wonderful secret.

"What's wrong with you?" Cecile finally asked.

Jenny let out a short burst of air and sat up straight. "The reason why my mother made me get dressed like this is because she's worried I might do too much with you. Well, not you, I mean, with your sister. Things that would get me in trouble." The words tumbled out in a rush. "Natalie, I mean." She looked at Cecile with suspense-filled eyes. "My mother says Natalie's fast."

Cecile had sat up very straight, too. "Fast at what?" she said.

"Kissing. William came home with lipstick on his face last night. He told my mother it was Natalie's." Jenny's eyes were gleaming. "He had a dark mark on his neck, too."

"And he told your mother it was Natalie's fault?" Cecile said, feeling anger and amazement rising inside. "Why would he tell her anything?"

"She asked." Jenny had slipped back into her prim-and-proper posture. "He always tells my mother things when she asks."

"Why didn't your mother say William was fast?"

Jenny's eyes opened wide. "Because he's not . . . I mean, I don't know," Jenny sputtered. "My mother said boys are supposed to want to kiss girls at his age, but that girls are supposed to be slower and wait. Natalie's only fourteen, you know."

"I know how old my sister is," Cecile said. "And your mother's an idiot."

"That's not very nice."

"Well, she is. Saying girls should be slower than boys. Do *you* think girls should be slower than boys?"

"No . . ."

"Neither do I. And I think your brother's an idiot, too, for telling your mother. What kind of tattletale is he?"

"A tattletale with a hickey on his neck," Jenny said. She clamped both hands over her mouth, her eyes laughing.

"Oh, gross," Cecile said. It was such a stupid picture, such a silly thing, to think of horrible William with his horrible neck, telling his mommy everything. She suddenly felt like laughing, too. "I'm so sick of all this ridiculous conversation about girls and boys, aren't you?"

Jenny nodded.

"Listen." Cecile leaned forward. "I'm going to go and get you a T-shirt and a pair of shorts so we can do something fun."

"You mean, you want me to change out here?" Jenny cried, looking excitedly around. "In the open?"

"No one can see. I'll bring a hanger, too," Cecile said as she stood up, "so you can hang up your dress."

"Are you sure?"

"Sure I'm sure," Cecile said. "Your mother never goes out of the house, anyway, so she won't see you. And no one else cares."

"Okay." Jenny stood up and started unbuttoning her dress. "But hurry!" she said.

"I'll be right back." Cecile stopped outside the bush. "You get to choose. Where do you want to go?"

There was no hesitation in Jenny's voice when she said, "Under the dock."

"They're gone," Cecile announced as she came onto the terrace.

"Thank god." Natalie lowered her magazine and let her head fall back against the chaise. "I'm not going to do a single thing for the rest of our vacation except lie around and work on my tan."

"Why?" Cecile asked as she sat down. "Was it really so hard getting William to fall in love with you?"

"Hah, in love," Natalie scoffed. "I hear Harry's coming home. What'd I tell you?"

"At least Mom won't be in a rotten mood for the rest of our vacation."

"True."

Cecile watched her sister for a minute. Natalie's face was pale, but the dark circles under her eyes were gone. She looked bleached out but beautiful.

"Mrs. Cahoon told William you're fast, you know," Cecile said.

"She did?"

"Yep."

"God, that is so Cahoony," said Natalie.

"Cahoony?"

Natalie sat up. "Do you know what William does?" she said.

"What?"

Natalie swung her feet around and leaned forward with her elbows on her knees. "He carries a tiny notebook around with him all the time to keep track of his expenses. His father told him that if he started the habit when William was young, it would stand him in good stead for the rest of his life."

"'Good stead?'" Cecile repeated.

"William writes down every single thing he buys, every day: gas, oil for the car, snacks, magazines . . ." Natalie's eyes had some of their old sparkle. "He told me he even writes down 'personal items.' That's what he called them." She couldn't hold it in any longer; she laughed.

"What are those?" Cecile said.

"I don't know. He was too embarrassed to tell me."

They looked at each other and giggled.

"Can you imagine being married to a person like that?" Natalie said, sighing as she lay back in her chaise.

"I can't imagine even *kissing* him," Cecile said.

"Ugh. Please." Natalie closed her eyes and immediately opened them again. "Let's make a pact. We will never say the words 'William Cahoon' again. Deal?"

"Deal."

"I have a great idea," Natalie said. She shut her magazine with a decisive snap. "Let's ask Sheba to make us a picnic, and then you and I will go to the beach near the club and lie around all afternoon and eat and swim."

"Okay."

"You can't tell Jack, or Lucy, or anyone, that we're going," Natalie said as she stood up.

"Good idea."

"And whatever you do," Natalie instructed as she

led the way to the door, "don't start acting all interested in every baby we see on the beach, the way you always do, or we'll end up baby-sitting all afternoon."

"Right." Cecile followed her sister into the house. "And you can't start making eyes, or flirting, or even talking to any boy, no matter how gorgeous he is."

"I can't?" Natalie said, stopping.

"No, you can't." Cecile gave her a push to get her moving again. "And wear your tank suit like mine so we'll look like twins."

"In your dreams," Natalie said with a haughty toss of her hair as she knocked in a friendly way against Cecile's shoulder. "You go get dressed. I'll check with Sheba. And not a word to the others!" she called as Cecile started up the stairs.

"Not a word to us about what?" asked Jack, who was playing with his little men in the upstairs hall.

"None of your beeswax," Cecile sang.

"Powpowpow," said Jack.

Chapter Fifteen

Cecile leaned against the sill of the bathroom window brushing her teeth. The early morning air was hot and still. A bee flitting in front of the window hung suspended in midair for a long second, buzzing loudly, before it abruptly bounced off the screen and veered crazily off in the opposite direction.

Sheba had gone home for her day off yesterday. Cecile had been coming back from the dock when she saw her on the front steps with Mr. Peabody. He was joking and talking as he put Sheba's suitcase into the trunk of his car. Whatever he said made Sheba slap him on the arm and laugh. It was the sound of that laugh, so full and easy, as if Mr. Peabody had said something he wouldn't have liked someone like Cecile to hear, that had made Cecile step back into the shadow of the oak, suddenly shy.

Who was this stranger, she wondered uneasily, who looked so vibrant and glamorous in her sleeveless red dress with a wide white belt, her normally straight hair so alive with waves and curls? Surely her Sheba had never worn high heels as pointy and tall; the calves of her legs had never been so muscular. It wasn't the Sheba who Cecile knew.

She'd shivered, suddenly, as she stood there, to think what this Sheba might do or say if she were to pass Cecile on the street. Would she love Cecile still, or would she walk right past?

Cecile had hung back as Sheba and Mr. Peabody got into the car, slammed the doors, started up the engine, and drove away. She wished now that she'd said good-bye. That she'd been sure enough, somehow, to tell Sheba to have a good time.

Slowly Cecile rinsed her mouth and put her toothbrush back in its holder and walked into her bedroom. What harm could there be in putting on that silly bra again? She had to get used to it sometime. Better wear it to the club and see how it felt.

"Cecile! Natalie!" Her mother's voice sounded exactingly from the driveway outside. "We're meeting Granddad and Dad at noon!"

"The only reason I'm late is because you took so long in there," Natalie said, pushing past Cecile when they met on the stairs. "Tell Mom I'll be a minute."

Their mother was standing beside the car. Lucy and Jack were already in the back. "Would you please run to the dock and see if Lucy left her sandals there?" her mother said when Cecile appeared. "Check in the box in the boathouse in case someone found them and dumped them there."

"Okay." Cecile dropped her towel in through the front window and set off.

"And hurry!" her mother called as she ran onto the drive.

Trust Lucy, Cecile thought as she ran. Mom ought to tie her shoes to her feet, the way she leaves them everywhere. She ran down the steps to the dock, into the boathouse, and almost into Stefan's open arms.

"Whoa," he cried, backing up. "Are you looking

for these?" He held out Lucy's sandals. "I figured someone would be back for them."

"Thanks." Cecile took the sandals quickly, as if fearing he was using them as bait to grab her, and ducked her head. He was standing so close. She couldn't look him in the face.

"You're Cecile, right?"

She took a step back and looked up. "How do you know?"

"Jack told me."

"He did? Why?"

Stefan picked up a large metal scoop from the table beside the freezer and opened the door. "I asked him," he said as he started scooping up ice and dumping it into a bucket at his feet. "I wanted to know which one of his sisters would have come down here a few nights ago and done what looked like a cross between a war dance and a cheerleading exercise." Stefan shot her an amused look as he dumped the last scoop into the bucket and let the freezer door slam shut. "Jack said, 'It had to be Cecile.'" He laughed.

"It *was* a war dance, now that you mention it," Cecile said, lifting her chin.

"I figured as much." Stefan picked up the bucket. "But that little 'blue team' bit at the end kind of threw me off."

He had a friendly laugh. Cecile could feel herself grinning.

"You might want to look around inside there some more," he said with a jerk of his head at the boathouse. "There are quite a few buckets and shovels."

"We leave those here every summer," Cecile said. "For the next year."

"Right. You would."

"Are you coming back next year?"

"As a matter of fact, I'm leaving today, for good," Stefan said. "Captain Stone and I are taking a group down to Florida this afternoon. I'll fly home from there. I've got to get ready to go to college in a few weeks."

"College? Wow. You're really old."

She blushed to hear how young she sounded, but

Stefan only laughed. "Ancient," he said. He put a hand in the middle of his back and hunched over, limping like an old man with a cane.

"Need help with that, old man?" Cecile said.

"No sirree," Stefan said, shooting back up. "Not from you. You make me nervous."

Cecile laughed.

"It was nice meeting you, Cecile," Stefan said. "Say good-bye to Jack for me."

"Bye, Stefan." Cecile floated up the stairs, supremely happy. He was so terribly normal and nice. Best of all, now he'd be gone, and the dock would be hers again. "Oh, and Stefan," she cried, whirling around when she got to the parking area. Stefan, halfway down the dock, turned. "I'll never be too much work!" Cecile cried.

"What?" Stefan's face went from blank to surprised. Then he smiled a huge smile and shot her a neat salute. Cecile saluted back and ran up the drive on winged feet. Flinging Lucy's sandals into the backseat, she cried, "Here you go, Lucy!" and ran around the front of the car. "I've decided," she said as she slid into the front seat next to her mother, "I'm willing to take tennis lessons, but I draw the line at golf."

"That's my seat, Cecile," Natalie called as she came out the front door. "Move it."

"First come, first served," Cecile said.

"Natalie, get in the car, please," their mother said.

"Stefan said good-bye," Cecile told Jack over her shoulder as Natalie sulkily slammed the back door. "He's leaving today, for good."

"I know," said Jack.

"Why didn't you tell me you knew him?" Cecile said.

"You didn't ask me."

"Who's Stefan?" said Natalie.

"No one you know," Cecile said.

"No one I want to know, you mean."

"Same thing."

"Brat." Natalie leaned forward to jab Cecile in the back.

"Same to you."

"When'd you get a bra, by the way?" Natalie

asked, rubbing her hand on Cecile's shoulder.

"Ages ago." Cecile sat forward, out of her reach.

"Liar. You're such a liar, Cecile. Mom, did you buy it for her?"

"Natalie, enough. How would you like it if Cecile were to discuss your personal business in front of everyone?" Mrs. Thompson said. "I don't want another word out of either one of you."

Natalie poked Cecile in the back again, but it felt good.

"Wait for me. I have to go to the bathroom," Natalie said, resting her tennis racket against the wall of the ladies' changing rooms before she went inside. Cecile stood idly bouncing a ball on the sidewalk with her racket.

"Hi, Cecile."

Cecile turned. Whit was coming from the direction of the golf course with three boys. When he stopped in front of her, they clustered around behind, shifting from foot to foot and grinning.

"Hi." Cecile quickly caught the ball and held it

awkwardly against her stomach with one hand to stop it from bouncing.

"Are you up for another game?" said Whit.

"Yeah, maybe you'll get caught this time," one of the boys muttered. The other boys laughed.

"Go on, you guys," Whit said sharply. "I'll catch up with you." He and Cecile stood looking at each other as they walked off. "They didn't mean it," Whit said when they were gone.

"It's all right," Cecile said. "When are you playing?"

"Thursday night. Want to come?"

"I don't know if I can."

"Oh. Okay." Whit looked in the direction his friends had gone, then back at Cecile. "Those guys didn't mean it, you know. I wouldn't let them do anything, anyway."

"They'd be sorry if they tried."

"Yeah." Whit nodded. "I believe that."

Their grins came and went.

"Well," Whit said after neither one said anything for a minute. "Maybe I'll see you on Thursday and maybe I won't."

"Right."

"Okay. Well, bye."

"Bye."

Cecile dumbly watched him walk to catch up with his friends. Say something, say something, say something, you idiot! Something so he knows you don't hate him, but not something that'll let him know you think he's cute.

"Whit, wait!" Cecile ran after him, she didn't care. Whit had stopped to wait for her. "I'd love to play again," she said in a rush when she caught up, "but I can't. Not on Thursday, I mean. My brother's coming home from Canada on Thursday. We're having a family party at my grandfather's. I have to be there."

"Oh. Great!" Whit's smile was as wonderful as his eyes. "I mean, it's not great that you can't come, but it's great. Great that your brother's coming home, I mean. But I wish you could play."

"I will the next time," Cecile said.

"You will?"

"Sure."

"Great! I'll let you know."

"Great." Would they ever stop repeating themselves!

"Well, bye, I guess," said Whit. "Have fun at your party."

"Have fun at your game." Cecile worked hard to keep her grin from splitting her face in two as she walked, backward, away from him. "Don't do any more damage to the you-know-what!" she called.

Whit turned around and grinned. "We won't!"

"Who was that?" Natalie asked as she came up behind.

"A boy."

"I know he was a boy," said Natalie. "What did he want?"

"Nothing."

"He didn't ask you on a date?"

"Are you nuts?"

"I guess that is nuts."

"Anyway, I'm not you," Cecile said. "I can have boys as friends."

"That's probably all you'll ever have them as."

"Suits me."

"Good thing."

* * *

A seagull flying overhead a short time later would have seen two young girls playing tennis on the last court in a long row of clay courts behind the imposing brick clubhouse that overlooked the bay.

The air was punctuated with the satisfying *thonk* of tennis balls against tightly strung rackets, and the *thwack* of golf balls as they hurtled their way on an improbable journey through the air in search of one tiny, specific hole.

The voices of the two girls carry through the air, too.

"Fifteen-love!" called the girl with the blond hair after a particularly neat serve.

"Love-hate!" the dark-haired girl called back.

"Cecile, that's the way you keep score."

"Natalie, I told you I wouldn't play if we keep score."

The blond girl's shots are proficient, but cold. The dark-haired girl's shots are random, but strong.

From the gull's clear vantage, it looks like an even match.